SUNRISE ON M

SUNRISE ON MERCURY

Thirteen Stories

by

ROBERT SILVERBERG

LONDON

VICTOR GOLLANCZ LTD

1983

ACKNOWLEDGMENTS

Sunrise on Mercury, copyright © 1957 by Columbia Publications, Inc.

Why?, copyright © 1957 by Columbia Publications, Inc.

There Was An Old Woman—, copyright © 1958 by Royal Publications, Inc.

Alaree, copyright © 1958 by Candar Publishing Co.

Going Down Smooth, © 1968 by Galaxy Publishing Corporation

The Man Who Never Forgot, copyright © 1957 by Fantasy House, Inc.

World of a Thousand Colors, copyright © 1957 by Headline Publications, Inc.

The Day the Founder Died, copyright © 1974 by Roger Elwood

The Artifact Business, copyright © 1957 by King-Size Publications

The Silent Colony, copyright © 1954 by Columbia Publications, Inc.

The Four, copyright © 1958 by Columbia Publications, Inc.

Precedent, copyright © 1957 by Street & Smith Publications, Inc.

After the Myths Went Home, copyright © 1969 by Mercury Press, Inc.

British Library Cataloguing in Publication Data
Silverberg, Robert
   Sunrise on Mercury.
   I. Title
   813'.54[F]   PS3569.I472

ISBN 0-575-03217-0

Photoset and printed in Great Britain by
Photobooks (Bristol) Limited
Barton Manor, St Philips, Bristol

In Memory of Ted Carnell

Contents

Sunrise on Mercury

Nine million miles to the sunward of Mercury, with the *Leverrier* swinging into the series of spirals that would bring it down on the solar system's smallest world, Second Astrogator Lon Curtis decided to end his life.

Curtis had been lounging in a webfoam cradle waiting for the landing to be effected; his job in the operation was over, at least until the *Leverrier*'s landing-jacks touched Mercury's blistered surface. The ship's efficient sodium-coolant system negated the efforts of the swollen sun visible through the rear screen. For Curtis and his seven shipmates, no problems presented themselves; they had only to wait while the autopilot brought the ship down for man's second landing on Mercury.

Flight Commander Harry Ross was sitting near Curtis when he noticed the sudden momentary stiffening of the astrogator's jaws. Curtis abruptly reached for the control nozzle. From the spinnerets that had spun the webfoam came a quick green burst of dissolving fluorochrene; the cradle vanished. Curtis stood up.

"Going somewhere?" Ross asked.

Curtis' voice was harsh. "Just—just taking a walk."

Ross returned his attention to his microbook for a moment as Curtis walked away. There was the ratchety sound of a bulkhead dog being manipulated, and Ross felt a momentary chill as the cooler air of the superrefrigerated reactor compartment drifted in.

He punched a stud, turning the page. Then—

What the hell is he doing in the reactor compartment?

The autopilot would be controlling the fuel flow, handling it down to the milligram, in a way no human system could. The reactor was primed for the landing, the fuel was stoked, the compartment was dogged shut. No one—least of all a second astrogator—had any business going back there.

Ross had the foam cradle dissolved in an instant, and was on his feet a moment later. He dashed down the companionway and through the open bulkhead door into the coolness of the reactor compartment.

Curtis was standing by the converter door, toying with the release-tripper. As Ross approached, he saw the astrogator get the door open and put one foot to the chute that led downship to the nuclear pile.

"Curtis, you idiot! Get away from there! You'll kill us all!"

The astrogator turned, looked blankly at Ross for an instant, and drew up his other foot. Ross leaped.

He caught Curtis' booted foot in his hands, and despite a barrage of kicks from the astrogator's free boot, managed to drag Curtis off the chute. The astrogator tugged and pulled, attempting to break free. Ross saw the man's pale cheeks quivering; Curtis had cracked, but thoroughly.

Grunting, Ross yanked Curtis away from the yawning reactor chute and slammed the door shut. He dragged him out into the main section again and slapped him, hard.

"Why'd you want to do that? Don't you know what your mass would do to the ship if it got into the converter? You know the fuel intake's been calibrated already; 180 extra pounds and we'd arc right into the sun. What's wrong with you, Curtis?"

The astrogator fixed unshaking, unexpressive eyes on Ross. "I want to die," he said simply. "Why couldn't you let me die?"

He wanted to die. Ross shrugged, feeling a cold tremor run down his back. There was no guarding against this disease.

Just as aqualungers beneath the sea's surface suffered from *l'ivresse des grandes profondeurs*—rapture of the deeps—and knew no cure for the strange, depth-induced drunkenness that caused them to remove their breathing tubes fifty fathoms below, so did spacemen run the risk of this nameless malady, this inexplicable urge to self-destruction.

It struck anywhere. A repairman wielding a torch on a

recalcitrant strut of an orbiting wheel might abruptly rip open his facemask and drink vacuum; a radioman rigging an antenna on the skin of his ship might suddenly cut his line, fire his directional pistol, and send himself drifting away. Or a second astrogator might decide to climb into the converter.

Psych Officer Spangler appeared, an expression of concern fixed on his smooth pink face. "Trouble?"

Ross nodded. "Curtis. Tried to jump into the fuel chute. He's got it, Doc."

Spangler rubbed his cheek and said: "They always pick the best times, dammit. It's swell having a psycho on a Mercury run."

"That's the way it is," Ross said wearily. "Better put him in stasis till we get home. I'd hate to have him running loose, looking for different ways of doing himself in."

"Why can't you let me die?" Curtis asked. His face was bleak. "Why'd you have to stop me?"

"Because, you lunatic, you'd have killed all the rest of us by your fool dive into the converter. Go walk out the airlock if you want to die—but don't take us with you."

Spangler glared warningly at him. "Harry—"

"Okay," Ross said. "Take him away."

The psychman led Curtis within. The astrogator would be given a tranquilising injection and locked in an insoluble webfoam jacket for the rest of the journey. There was a chance he could be restored to sanity once they returned to Earth, but Ross knew that the astrogator would go straight for the nearest method of suicide the moment he was released aboard the ship.

Scowling, Ross turned away. A man spends his boyhood dreaming about space, he thought, spends four years at the Academy, and two more making dummy runs. Then he finally gets out where it counts and he cracks up. Curtis was an astrogation machine, not a normal human being; and he had just disqualified himself permanently from the only job he knew how to do.

Ross shivered, feeling chill despite the bloated bulk of the sun filling the rear screen. It could happen to anyone . . . even him. He thought of Curtis lying in a foam cradle somewhere in the back of the ship, blackly thinking over and over again, *I want to die*, while

Doc Spangler muttered soothing things at him. A human being was really a frail form of life.

Death seemed to hang over the ship; the gloomy aura of Curtis' suicide-wish polluted the atmosphere.

Ross shook his head and punched down savagely on the signal to prepare for deceleration. Mercury's sharp globe bobbed up ahead. He spotted it through the front screen.

They were approaching the tiny planet middle-on. He could see the neat division now: the brightness of Sunside, that unapproachable inferno where zinc ran in rivers, and the icy blackness of Darkside, dull with its unlit plains of frozen CO_2.

Down the heart of the planet ran the Twilight Belt, that narrow area of not-cold and not-heat where Sunside and Darkside met to provide a thin band of barely tolerable territory, a ring nine thousand miles in circumference and ten or twenty miles wide.

The *Leverrier* plunged planetward. Ross allowed his jangled nerves to grow calm. The ship was in the hands of the autopilot; the orbit, of course, was precomputed, and the analog banks in the drive were serenely following the taped program, bringing the ship toward its destination smack in the middle of—

My God!

Ross went cold from head to toe. The precomputed tape had been fed to the analog banks—had been prepared by—had been entirely the work of—

Curtis.

A suicidal madman had worked out the *Leverrier*'s landing program.

Ross began to shake. How easy it would have been, he thought, for death-bent Curtis to work out an orbit that would plant the *Leverrier* in a smoking river of molten lead—or in the mortuary chill of Darkside.

His false security vanished. There was no trusting the automatic pilot; they'd have to risk a manual landing.

Ross jabbed down on the communicator button. "I want Brainerd," he said hoarsely.

The first astrogator appeared a few seconds later, peering in curiously. "What goes, Captain?"

"We've just carted your assistant Curtis off to the pokey. He tried to jump into the converter."

"He—"

Ross nodded. "Attempted suicide. I got to him in time. But in view of the circumstances, I think we'd better discard the tape you had him prepare and bring the ship down manually, yes?"

The first astrogator moistened his lips. "That sounds like a good idea."

"Damn right it is," Ross said, glowering.

As the ship touched down Ross thought, *Mercury is two hells in one.*

It was the cold, ice-bound kingdom of Dante's deepest pit—and it was also the brimstone empire of another conception. The two met, fire and frost, each hemisphere its own kind of hell.

He lifted his head and flicked a quick glance at the instrument panel above his deceleration cradle. The dials all checked: weight placement was proper, stability 100 percent, external temperature a manageable 108° F., indicating they had made their descent a little to the sunward of the Twilight Belt's exact middle. It had been a sound landing.

He snapped on the communicator. "Brainerd?"

"All okay, Captain."

"Manual landing?"

"I had to," the astrogator said. "I ran a quick check on Curtis' tape, and it was all cockeyed. The way he had us coming in, we'd have grazed Mercury's orbit by a whisker and kept on going—straight into the sun. Nice?"

"Very sweet," Ross said. "But don't be too hard on the kid. He didn't *want* to go psycho. Good landing, anyway. We seem to be pretty close to the centre of the Twilight Belt, and that's where I feel most comfortable."

He broke the contact and unwebbed himself. Over the shipwide circuit he called all hands fore, double pronto.

The men got there quickly enough—Brainerd first, then Doc Spangler, followed by Accumulator Tech Krinsky and the three other crewmen. Ross waited until the entire group had assembled.

They were looking around curiously for Curtis. Crisply, Ross told them, "Astrogator Curtis is going to miss this meeting. He's aft in the psycho bin. Luckily, we can shift without him on this tour."

He waited until the implications of that statement had sunk in. The men seemed to adjust to it well enough, he thought: momentary expressions of dismay, shock, even horror quickly faded from their faces.

"All right," he said. "Schedule calls for us to put in some thirty-two hours of extravehicular activity on Mercury. Brainerd, how does that check with our location?"

The astrogator frowned and made some mental calculations. "Current position is a trifle to the sunward edge of the Twilight Belt; but as I figure it, the sun won't be high enough to put the Fahrenheit much above 120 for at least a week. Our suits can handle that temperature with ease."

"Good. Llewellyn, you and Falbridge break out the radar inflaters and get the tower set up as far to the east as you can go without getting roasted. Take the crawler, but be sure to keep an eye on the thermometer. We've only got one heatsuit, and that's for Krinsky."

Llewellyn, a thin, sunken-eyed spaceman, shifted uneasily. "How far to the east do you suggest, sir?"

"The Twilight Belt covers about a quarter of Mercury's surface," Ross said. "You've got a strip forty-seven degrees wide to move around in—but I don't suggest you go much more than twenty-five miles or so. It starts getting hot after that. And keeps going up."

Ross turned to Krinsky. In many ways the accumulator tech was the expedition's key man: it was his job to check the readings on the pair of solar accumulators that had been left here by the first expedition. He was to measure the amount of stress created by solar energies here, so close to the source of radiation, study force-lines operating in the strange magnetic field of the little world, and reprime the accumulators for further testing by the next expedition.

Krinsky was a tall, powerfully built man, the sort of man who could stand up to the crushing weight of a heatsuit almost cheerfully. The heatsuit was necessary for prolonged work in the Sunside zone, where the accumulators were mounted—and even a giant like Krinsky could stand the strain for only a few hours at a time.

"When Llewellyn and Falbridge have the radar tower set up, Krinsky, get into your heatsuit and be ready to move. As soon as we've got the accumulator station located, Dominic will drive you as far east as possible and drop you off. The rest is up to you. Watch your step. We'll be telemetering your readings, but we'd like to have you back alive."

"Yes, sir."

"That's about it," Ross said. "Let's get rolling."

Ross's own job was purely administrative—and as the men of his crew moved busily about their allotted tasks, he realised unhappily that he himself was condemned to temporary idleness. His function was that of overseer; like the conductor of a symphony orchestra, he played no instrument himself and was on hand mostly to keep the group moving in harmony toward the finish.

Everyone was in motion. Now he had only to wait.

Llewellyn and Falbridge departed, riding the segmented, thermo-resistant crawler that had traveled to Mercury in the belly of the *Leverrier*. Their job was simple: they were to erect the inflatable plastic radar tower out toward the sunward sector. The tower that the first expedition had left had long since librated into a Sunside zone and been liquefied; the plastic base and parabola, covered with a light reflective surface of aluminum, could hardly withstand the searing heat of Sunside.

Out there, it got up to 700° when the sun was at its closest. The eccentricities of Mercury's orbit accounted for considerable temperature variations on Sunside, but the thermometer never showed lower than 300° out there, even during aphelion. On Darkside, there was less of a temperature range; mostly the temperature hovered not far from absolute zero, and frozen drifts of heavy gases covered the surface of the land.

From where he stood, Ross could see neither Sunside nor Darkside. The Twilight Belt was nearly a thousand miles broad, and as the little planet dipped in its orbit the sun would first slide above the horizon, then slip back. For a twenty-mile strip through the heart of the Belt, the heat of Sunside and the cold of Darkside canceled out into a fairly stable, temperate climate; for five hundred miles on either side, the Twilight Belt gradually trickled toward the areas of extreme cold and raging heat.

It was a strange and forbidding planet. Humans could endure it for only a short time; it was worse than Mars, worse than the Moon. The sort of life capable of living permanently on Mercury was beyond Ross's powers of imagination. Standing outside the *Leverrier* in his spacesuit, he nudged the chin control that lowered a sheet of optical glass. He peered first toward Darkside, where he thought he saw a thin line of encroaching black—only illusion, he knew—and then toward Sunside.

In the distance, Llewellyn and Falbridge were erecting the spidery parabola that was the radar tower. He could see the clumsy shape outlined against the sky now—and behind it? A faint line of brightness rimming the bordering peaks? Illusion also, he knew. Brainerd had calculated that the sun's radiance would not be visible here for a week. And in a week's time they'd be back on Earth.

He turned to Krinsky. "The tower's nearly up. They'll be coming in with the crawler any minute. You'd better get ready to make your trip."

As the accumulator tech swung up the handholds and into the ship, Ross's thoughts turned to Curtis. The young astrogator had talked excitedly of seeing Mercury all the way out—and now that they were actually here, Curtis lay in a web of foam deep within the ship, moodily demanding the right to die.

Krinsky returned, now wearing the insulating bulk of the heatsuit over his standard rebreathing outfit. He looked more like a small tank than a man. "Is the crawler approaching, sir?"

"I'll check."

Ross adjusted the lensplate in his mask and narrowed his eyes. It seemed to him that the temperature had risen a little. Another illusion? He squinted into the distance.

His eyes picked out the radar tower far off toward Sunside. He gasped.

"Something the matter?" Krinsky asked.

"I'll say!" Ross squeezed his eyes tight shut and looked again.

And—yes—the newly erected radar tower was drooping soggily and beginning to melt. He saw two tiny figures racing madly over the flat, pumice-covered ground to the silvery oblong that was the crawler. And—impossibly—the first glow of an unmistakable brightness was beginning to shimmer on the mountains behind the tower.

The sun was rising—a week ahead of schedule!

Ross ran back into the ship, followed by the lumbering figure of Krinsky. In the airlock, obliging mechanical hands descended to ease him out of his spacesuit; signaling to Krinsky to keep the heatsuit on, he dashed through into the main cabin.

"Brainerd! Brainerd! Where in hell are you?"

The senior astrogator appeared, looking puzzled. "What's up, Captain?"

"Look out the screen," Ross said in a strangled voice. "Look at the radar tower!"

"It's—*melting*," Brainerd said, astonished. "But that's—that's—"

"I know. It's impossible." Ross glanced at the instrument panel. External temperature had risen to 112°—a jump of four degrees. And as he watched it glided up to 114°.

It would take a heat of at least 500° to melt the radar tower that way. Ross squinted at the screen and saw the crawler come swinging dizzily toward them: Llewellyn and Falbridge were still alive, then—though they probably had had a good cooking out there. The temperature outside the ship was up to 116°. It would probably be near 200° by the time the two men returned.

Angrily, Ross whirled to face the astrogator. "I thought you were bringing us down in the safety strip," he snapped. "Check your figures again and find out where the hell we *really* are. Then work out a blasting orbit, fast. That's the *sun* coming up over those hills."

The temperature had reached 120°. The ship's cooling system would be able to keep things under control and comfortable until about 250°; beyond that, there was danger of an overload. The crawler continued to draw near. It was probably hellish inside the little land car, Ross thought.

His mind weighed alternatives. If the external temperature went much over 250°, he would run the risk of wrecking the ship's cooling system by waiting for the two in the crawler to arrive. There was some play in the system, but not much. He decided he'd give them until it hit 275° to get back. If they didn't make it by then, he'd have to take off without them. It was foolish to try to save two lives at the risk of six. External temperature had hit 130°. Its rate of increase was jumping rapidly.

The ship's crew knew what was going on now. Without the need of direct orders from Ross, they were readying the *Leverrier* for an emergency blastoff.

The crawler inched forward. The two men weren't much more than ten miles away now; and at an average speed of forty miles an hour they'd be back within fifteen minutes. Outside the temperature was 133°. Long fingers of shimmering sunlight stretched toward them from the horizon.

Brainerd looked up from his calculation. "I can't work it. The damned figures don't come out."

"Huh?"

"I'm trying to compute our location—and I can't do the arithmetic. My head's all foggy."

What the hell. This was where a captain earned his pay, Ross thought. "Get out of the way," he said brusquely. "Let me do it."

He sat down at the desk and started figuring. He saw Brainerd's hasty notations scratched out everywhere. It was as if the astrogator had totally forgotten how to do his job.

Let's see, now. If we're—

He tapped out figures on the little calculator. But as he worked he saw that what he was doing made no sense. His mind felt bleary and strange; he couldn't seem to handle the elementary computations at all. Looking up, he said, "Tell Krinsky to get down there and make himself ready to help those men out of the crawler when they show up. They're probably half cooked."

Temperature 146°. He looked down at the calculator. Damn: it shouldn't be that hard to do simple trigonometry, should it?

Doc Spangler appeared. "I cut Curtis free," he announced. "He isn't safe during takeoff in that cradle."

From within came a steady mutter. "Just let me die . . . just let me die . . ."

"Tell him he's likely to get his wish," Ross murmured. "If I can't manage to work out a blastoff orbit we're all going to fry right here."

"How come you're doing it? What's the matter with Brainerd?"

"Choked up. Couldn't make sense of his own figures. And come to think of it, I'm not doing so well myself."

Fingers of fog seemed to wrap around his mind. He glanced at the dial. Temperature 152° outside. That gave the boys in the crawler 123° to get back here . . . or was it 321°? He was confused, utterly bewildered.

Doc Spangler looked peculiar too. The psych officer wore an odd frown. "I feel very lethargic suddenly," Spangler declared. "I know I really should get back to Curtis, but—"

The madman was keeping up a steady babble inside. The part of Ross's mind that still could think clearly realised that if left unattended Curtis was capable of doing almost anything.

Temperature 158°.

The crawler seemed to be getting nearer. On the horizon the radar tower was melting into a crazy shambles.

There was a shriek. "Curtis!" Ross yelled, his mind hurriedly returning to awareness. He ran aft, with Spangler close behind.

Too late.

Curtis lay on the floor in a bloody puddle. He had found a pair of shears somewhere.

Spangler bent. "He's dead."

"Dead. Of course." Ross's brain felt totally clear now. At the moment of Curtis' death the fog had lifted. Leaving Spangler to attend to the body, he returned to the astrogation desk and glanced through the calculations he had been doing. Worthless. An idiotic mess.

With icy clarity he started again, and this time succeeded in determining their location. They had come down better than three hundred miles sunward of where they had thought they were landing. The instruments hadn't lied—but someone's eyes had. The orbit that Brainerd had so solemnly assured him was a "safe" one was actually almost as deadly as the one Curtis had computed.

He looked outside. The crawler had almost reached the ship. Temperature 167° out there. There was plenty of time. They would make it with a few minutes to spare, thanks to the warning they had received from the melting radar tower.

But why had it happened? There was no answer to that.

Gigantic in his heatsuit, Krinsky brought Llewellyn and Falbridge aboard. They peeled out of their spacesuits and wobbled around unsteadily for a moment before they collapsed. They were as red as newly boiled lobsters.

"Heat prostration," Ross said. "Krinsky, get them into takeoff cradles. Dominic, you in your suit yet?"

The spaceman appeared at the airlock entrance and nodded.

"Good. Get down there and drive the crawler into the hold. We can't afford to leave it here. Double-quick, and then we're blasting off. Brainerd, that new orbit ready?"

"Yes, sir."

The thermometer grazed 200. The cooling system was beginning to suffer—but it would not have to endure much more agony. Within minutes the *Leverrier* was lifting from Mercury's surface—minutes ahead of the relentless advance of the sun. The ship swung into a parking orbit not far above the planet's surface.

As they hung there, catching their breaths, just one thing occupied Ross's mind: *why?* Why had Brainerd's orbit brought them down in a danger zone instead of the safety strip? Why had both he and Brainerd been unable to compute a blasting pattern, the simplest of elementary astrogation techniques? And why had Spangler's wits utterly failed him—just long enough to let the unhappy Curtis kill himself?

Ross could see the same question reflected on everyone's face: why?

He felt an itchy feeling at the base of his skull. And suddenly an image forced its way across his mind and he had the answer.

He saw a great pool of molten zinc, lying shimmering between two jagged crests somewhere on Sunside. It had been there thousands of years; it would be there thousands, perhaps millions, of years from now.

Its surface quivered. The sun's brightness upon the pool was intolerable even to the mind's eye.

Radiation beat down on the pool of zinc—the sun's radiation, hard and unending. And then a new radiation, an electromagnetic emanation in a different part of the spectrum, carrying a meaningful message:

I want to die.

The pool of zinc stirred fretfully with sudden impulses of helpfulness.

The vision passed as quickly as it came. Stunned, Ross looked up. The expressions on the six faces surrounding him confirmed what he could guess.

"You all felt it too," he said.

Spangler nodded, then Krinsky and the rest of them.

"Yes," Krinsky said. "What the devil was it?"

Brainerd turned to Spangler. "Are we all nuts, Doc?"

The psych officer shrugged. "Mass hallucination . . . collective hypnosis . . ."

"No, Doc." Ross leaned forward. "You know it as well as I do. That thing was real. It's down there, out on Sunside."

"What do you mean?"

"I mean that wasn't any hallucination we had. That's something *alive* down there—or as close to alive as anything on Mercury can be." Ross's hands were shaking. He forced them to subside. "We've stumbled over something very big," he said.

Spangler stirred uneasily. "Harry—"

"No, I'm not out of my head! Don't you see—that thing down there, whatever it is, is sensitive to our thoughts! It picked up Curtis' godawful caterwauling the way a radar set grabs electromagnetic waves. His were the strongest thoughts coming through; so it acted on them and did its damndest to help Curtis get what he wanted."

"You mean by fogging our minds and deluding us into thinking we were in safe territory, when actually we were right near sunrise territory?"

"But why would it go to all that trouble?" Krinsky objected. "If it wanted to help poor Curtis kill himself, why didn't it just fix things so we came down right *in* Sunside. We'd cook a lot quicker that way."

"Originally it did," Ross said. "It helped Curtis set up a landing orbit that would have dumped us into the sun. But then it realised that the rest of us *didn't* want to die. It picked up the conflicting mental emanations of Curtis and the rest of us, and arranged things so that he'd die and we wouldn't." He shivered. "Once Curtis was out of the way, it acted to help the surviving crew members reach safety. If you'll remember, we were all thinking and moving a lot quicker the instant Curtis was dead."

"Damned if that's not so," Spangler said. "But—"

"What I want to know is, do we go back down?" Krinsky asked. "If that thing is what you say it is, I'm not so sure I want to go within reach of it again. Who knows what it might make us do this time?"

"It wants to help us," Ross said stubbornly. "It's not hostile. You aren't afraid of it, are you, Krinsky? I was counting on you to go out in the heatsuit and try to find it."

"Not me!"

Ross scowled. "But this is the first intelligent life-form man has ever found in the solar system. We can't just run away and hide." To Brainerd he said, "Set up an orbit that'll take us back down again—and this time put us down where we won't melt."

"I can't do it, sir," Brainerd said flatly.

"Can't?"

"Won't. I think the safest thing is for us to return to Earth at once."

"I'm ordering you."

"I'm sorry, sir."

Ross looked at Spangler. Llewellyn. Falbridge. Right around the circle. Fear was evident on every face. He knew what each of the men was thinking.

I don't want to go back to Mercury.

Six of them. One of him. And the helpful thing below.

They had outnumbered Curtis seven to one—but Curtis' mind

had radiated an unmixed death-wish. Ross knew he could never generate enough strength of thought to counteract the fear-driven thoughts of the other six.

Mutiny.

Somehow he did not care to speak the word aloud. Sometimes there were cases where a superior officer might legitimately be removed from command for the common good, and this might be one of them, he knew. But yet—

The thought of fleeing without even pausing to examine the creature below was intolerable to him. But there was only one ship, and either he or the six others would have to be denied.

Yet the pool had contrived to satisfy both the man who wished to die and those who wished to stay alive. Now, six wanted to return—but must the voice of the seventh be ignored?

You're not being fair to me, Ross thought, directing his angry outburst toward the planet below. *I want to see you. I want to study you. Don't let them drag me back to Earth so soon.*

When the *Leverrier* returned to Earth a week later, the six survivors of the Second Mercury Expedition all were able to describe in detail how a fierce death-wish had overtaken Second Astrogator Curtis and driven him to suicide. But not one of them could recall what had happened to Flight Commander Ross, or why the heatsuit had been left behind on Mercury.

Why?

And we left Capella XXII, after a six-month stay, and hopskipped across the galaxy to Dschubba, in the forehead of the Scorpion. And after the eight worlds of Dschubba had been seen and digested and recorded and classified, and after we had programmed all our material for transmission back to Earth, we moved on again, Brock and I.

We zeroed into warp and doublesqueaked into the star Pavo, which from Earth is seen to be the brightest star of the Peacock. And Pavo proved to be planetless, save for one ball of mud and methane a billion miles out; we chalked the mission off as unpromising, and moved on once again.

Brock was the coordinator; I, the fine-tooth man. He saw in patterns; I, in particular. We had been teamed for eleven years. We had visited seventy-eight stars and one hundred and sixty-three planets. The end was not quite in sight.

We hung in the grayness of warp, suspended neither in space nor in not-space, hovering in an interstice. Brock said, "I vote for Markab."

"Alpha Pegasi? No. I vote for Etamin."

But Gamma Draconis held little magic for him. He rubbed his angular hands through his tight-cropped hair and said, "The Wheel, then."

I nodded. "The Wheel."

The Wheel was our guide: not really a wheel so much as a map of the heavens in three dimensions, a lens of the galaxy, sprinkled brightly with stars. I pulled a switch; a beam of light lanced down from the ship's wall, needle-thin, playing against the Wheel. Brock seized the handle and imparted axial spin to the Wheel. Over and over for three, four, five rotations; then, stop. The light-beam stung Alphecca.

"Alphecca it will be," Brock said.

"Yes. Alphecca." I noted it in the log, and began setting up the coordinates on the drive. Brock was frowning uneasily.

"This failure to agree," he said. "This inability to decide on a matter so simple as our next destination—"

"Yes. Elucidate. Expound. Exegetise. What pattern do you see in that?"

Scowling he said, "Disagreement for the sake of disagreement is unhealthy. Conflict is valuable, but not for its own sake. It worries me."

"Perhaps we've been in space too long. Perhaps we should resign our commissions, leave the Exploratory Corps, return to Earth and settle there."

His face drained of blood. "No," he said. "No. No."

We emerged from warp within humming-distance of Alphecca, a bright star orbited by four worlds. Brock was playing calculus at the time; driblets of sweat glossed his face at each integration. I peered through the thick quartz of the observation panel and counted planets.

"Four worlds," I said. "One, two, three, and four."

I looked at him. His unfleshy face was tight with pain. After nearly a minute he said, "Pick one."

"Me?"

"*Pick one!*"

"Alphecca II."

"All right. We'll land there. I won't contest the point, Hammond. I *want* to land on Alphecca II." He grinned at me—a bright-eyed wild grin that I found unpleasant. But I saw what he was doing. He was easing a stress-pattern between us, eliminating a source of conflict before the chafing friction exploded. When two men live in a spaceship eleven years, such things are necessary.

Calmly and untensely I took a reading on Alphecca II. I sighted us in and actuated the computer. This was the way a landing was effected; this was the way Brock and I had effected one hundred sixty-three landings. The ion-drive exploded into life.

We dropped "downward." Alphecca II rose to meet us as our slim pale-green needle of a ship dived tail-first toward the world below.

The landing was routine. I sketched out a big 164 on my chart, and we donned spacesuits to make our preliminary explorations. Brock paused a moment at the airlock, smoothing the purple cloth of his suit, adjusting his air-intake, tightening his belt cincture. The corners of his mouth twitched nervously. Within the head-globe he looked frightened, and very tired.

I said, "You're not well. Maybe we should postpone our first look-see."

"Maybe we should go back to Earth, Hammond. And live in a beehive and breathe filthy gray soup." His voice was edged with bitter reproach. "Let's go outside," he said. He turned away, face shadowed morosely, and touched the stud that peeled back the airlock hatch.

I followed him into the lock and down the elevator. He was silent, stiff, reserved. I wished I had his talent for glimpsing patterns: this mood of his had probably been a long time building.

But I saw no cause for it. After eleven years, I thought, I should know him almost as well as I do myself. Or better. But no easy answers came, and I followed him out on to the exit stage and dropped gently down.

Landing One Six Four was entering the exploratory stage.

The ground spread out far to the horizon, a dull orange in color, rough in texture, pebbly, thick of consistency. We saw a few trees, bare-trunked, bluish. Green vines swarmed over the ground, twisted and gnarled.

Otherwise, nothing.

"Another uninhabited planet," I said. "That makes one hundred eight out of the hundred sixty-four."

"Don't be premature. You can't judge a world by a few acres. Land at a pole; extrapolate utter barrenness. It's not a valid pattern. Not enough evidence."

I cut him short. "Here's one time when I perceive a pattern. I perceive that this world's uninhabited. It's too damned quiet."

Chuckling, Brock said, "I incline to agree. But remember Adhara XI."

I remembered Adhara XI: the small, sandy world far from its primary, which seemed nothing but endless yellow sand dunes, rolling westward round and round the planet. We had joked about the desert-world, dry and parched, inhabited only by the restless dunes. But after the report was written, after our data were codified and flung through subspace toward Earth, we found the oasis on the eastern continent, the tiny garden of green things and sweet air that so sharply was unlike the rest of Adhara XI. I remembered sleek scaly creatures slithering through the crystal lake, and an indolent old worm sleeping beneath a heavy-fruited tree.

"Adhara XI is probably swarming with Earth tourists," I said. "Now that our amended report is public knowledge. I often think we should have concealed the oasis from Earth, and returned there ourselves when we grew tired of exploring the galaxy."

Brock's head snapped up sharply. He ripped a sprouting tip from a leathery vine and said, "*When* we grow tired? Hammond, aren't you tired already? Eleven years, a hundred sixty-four worlds?"

Now I saw the pattern taking fairly clear shape. I shook my head, throttling the conversation. "Let's get down the data, Brock. We can talk later."

We proceeded with the measurements of our particular sector of Alphecca II. We nailed down the dry vital statistics, bracketing them off so Earth could enter the neat figures in its giant catalog of explored worlds.

GRAVITY—*1.02 E.*

ATMOSPHERIC CONSTITUTION—ammonia/carbon dioxide Type ab7, unbreathable

ESTIMATED PLANETARY DIAMETER—.87 E.

INTELLIGENT LIFE—*none*

We filled out the standard forms, ran the standard tests, took the standard soil samples. Exploration had become a smooth mechanical routine. Our first tour lasted three hours. We wandered over the slowly rising hills, with the spaceship always at our backs, and Alphecca high beyond us. The dry soil crunched unpleasantly beneath our heavy boots.

Conversation was at a minimum. Brock and I rarely spoke when it was not absolutely necessary—and when we did speak, it was to let a tight, tense remark escape confinement, not to communicate anything. We shared too many silent memories. Eleven years and one hundred sixty-four planets. All Brock had to do was say *"Fomalhaut,"* or I *"Theta Eridani,"* and a train of associations and memories was set off in whose depths we could browse silently for hours and hours.

Alphecca II did not promise to be as memorable as those worlds. There would be nothing here to match the fantastic moonrise of Fomalhaut VI, the five hundred mirror-bright moons in stately procession through the sky, each glinting in a different hue. That moonrise had overwhelmed us four years ago, and remained yet bright. Alphecca II, dead world that it was, or rather world not yet alive, would leave no marks on our memories.

But bitterness was rising in Brock. I saw the pattern forming; I saw the question bubbling up through the layers of his mind, ready to be asked.

And on the fourth day, he let it be asked. After four days on Alphecca II, four days of staring at the grotesque twisted green shapes of the angular sprawling vines, four days of watching the lethargic fission of the pond protozoa who seemed to be the world's only animal life, Brock suddenly looked up at me.

He asked the shattering question that should never be asked.

"Why?" he said.

Eleven years and a hundred sixty-four worlds earlier, the seeds of that unanswered question had been sown. I was fresh out of the Academy, twenty-three, a tall, sharp-nosed boy with what some said was an irritatingly precise way of looking at things.

I should say that I bitterly resented being told I was coldly precise. People accused me of Teutonic heaviness. A girl I once had known said that to me, after a notably unsuccessful romance had come trailing to a halt. I recall turning to her, glaring at the light dusting of freckles across her nose, and telling her, "I have no Teutonic blood whatsoever. If you'll take the trouble to think of the probable Scandinavian derivation of my name—"

She slapped me.

Shortly after that, I met Brock—Brock, who at twenty-four was already the Brock I would know at thirty-five, harsh of face and voice, dark of complexion, with an expression of nervous wariness registering in his blue-black eyes always and ever. Brock never accused me of Teutonicism; he laughed when I cited some minor detail from memory, but the laugh was one of respect.

We were both Academy graduates; we both were restless. It showed in Brock's face, and I don't doubt it showed in mine. Earth was small and dirty and crowded, and each night the stars, those bright enough to glint through the haze and brightness of the cities, seemed to mock at us.

Brock and I gravitated naturally together. We shared a room in Appalachia North, we shared a library planchet, we shared reading-tapes and music-discs and occasionally lovers. And eight weeks after my twenty-third birthday, seven weeks before Brock's twenty-fourth, we hailed a cab and invested our last four coins in a trip downtown to the Administration of External Exploration.

There, we spoke to a bland-faced, smiling man with one leg prosthetic—he boasted of it—and his left hand a waxy synthetic one. "I got that way on Sirius VI," he told us. "But I'm an exception. Most of the exploration teams keep going for years and years, and nothing ever happens to them. McKees and Haugmuth have been out twenty-three years now. That's the record. We hear from them, every few months or so. They keep on going, farther and farther out."

Brock nodded. "Good. Give us the forms."

He signed first; I added my name below, finishing with a flourish. I stacked the triplicate forms neatly together and shoved them back at the half-synthetic recruiter.

"Excellent. Excellent. Welcome to the Corps."

He shook our hands, giving the hairy-knuckled right hand to Brock, the waxy left to me. I gripped it tightly, wondering if he could feel my grip.

Three days later we were in space, bound outward. In all the time since the original idea had sprung up unvoiced between us, neither Brock nor myself had paused to ask the damnable question.

Why?

We had joined the Corps. We had renounced Earth. Motive,

unstated. Or unknown. We let the matter lie dormant between us for eleven years, through a procession of strange and then less strange worlds.

Until Brock's agony broke forth to the surface. He destroyed eleven years of numb peace with one half-whispered syllable, there in the ship's lab our fourth morning on Alphecca II.

I looked at him for perhaps thirty seconds. Moistening my lips, I said, "What do you mean, Brock?"

"You know what I mean." The flat declarative tone was one of simple truth. "The one thing we haven't been asking ourselves all these years, because we knew we didn't have an answer for it and we *like* to have answers for things. Why are we here, on Alphecca II—with a hundred sixty-three visited worlds behind us?"

I shrugged. "You didn't have to start this, Brock." Outside the sun was climbing toward noon height, but I felt cold and dry, as if the ammonia atmosphere were seeping into the ship. It wasn't.

"No," he said. "I didn't have to start this. I could have let it fester for another eleven years. But it came popping out, and I want to settle it. We left Earth because we didn't like it there. Agreed?"

I nodded.

"But that's not *why* enough," he persisted. "Why do we explore? Why do we keep running from planet to planet, from one crazy airless ball to the next, out here where there are no people and no cities? Green crabs on Rigel V, sandfish on Caph. Dammit, Hammond, what are we looking for?"

Very calmly I said, "Ourselves, maybe?"

His face crinkled scornfully. "Foggy-eyed and imprecise, and you know it. We're not *looking* for ourselves out here. We're trying to *lose* ourselves. Eh?"

"No!"

"Admit it!"

I stared through the quartz window at the stiff, almost wooden vines that covered the pebbly ground. They seemed to be moving faintly, to be stretching their rigid bodies in a contraction of some sort. In a dull, tired voice, Brock said, "We left Earth because we couldn't cope with it. It was too crowded and too dirty for sensitive shrinking souls like us. We had the choice of withdrawing into shells and huddling there for eighty or ninety years, or else pulling up and leaving for space. We left. There's no society out here, just each other."

"We've adjusted to each other," I pointed out.

"So? Does that mean we could fit into Earth society? Would *you* want to go back? Remember the team—McKees and Haugmuth, is it?—who spent thirty-three years in space and came back. They were catatonic eight minutes after landing, the report said."

"Let me give you a simpler *why*," I ventured. "Why did you start griping all of a sudden? Why couldn't you hold it in?"

"That's not a simpler *why*. It's part of the same one. I came to an answer, and I didn't like it. I got the answer that we were out here because we couldn't make the grade on Earth."

"No!"

He smiled apologetically. "No? All right, then. Give me another answer. I *want* an answer, Hammond. I need one, now."

I pointed to the synthesiser. "Why don't you have a drink instead?"

"That comes later," he said somberly. "After I've given up trying to find out."

The stippling of fine details was becoming a sharp-focus picture. Brock—self-reliant Brock, self-contained, self-sufficient—had come to the end of his self-sufficiency. He had looked too deeply beneath the surface.

"At the age of eight," I began, "I asked my father what was outside the universe. That is, defining the universe as That Which Contains Everything, could there possibly be something or someplace outside its bounds? He looked at me for a minute or two, then laughed and told me not to worry about it. But I did worry about it. I stayed up half the night worrying about it, and my head hurt by morning. I never found out what was outside the universe."

"The universe is infinite," said Brock moodily. "Recurving in on itself, topologically—"

"Maybe. But I worried over it. I worried over First Cause. I worried all through my adolescence. Then I stopped worrying."

He smiled acidly. "You became a vegetable. You rooted yourself in the mud of your own ignorance, and decided not to pull loose because it was too painful. Am I right, Hammond?"

"No. I joined the Exploratory Corps."

I dreamed, that night, as I swung in my hammock. It was a vivid and unpleasant dream, which stayed with me well into the following morning as a sort of misshapen reality that had attached itself to me in the night.

I had been a long time falling asleep. Brock had brooded most of the day, and a long hike over the bleak tundra had done little to improve his mood. Toward nightfall he dialed a few drinks, inserted a disk of Sibelius in his ear, and sat staring glumly at the darkening sky outside the ship. Alphecca II was moonless. The night was the black of space, but the atmosphere blurred the neighboring stars.

I remember drifting off into a semisleep: a half-somnolence in which I was aware of Brock's harsh breathing to my left, but yet in which I had no volition, no control over my limbs. And after that state came sleep, and with it dreams.

The dream must have grown from Brock's bitter remark of earlier: *You became a vegetable. You rooted yourself in the mud of your own ignorance.*

I accepted the statement literally. Suddenly I *was* a vegetable, possessed of all my former faculties, but rooted in the soil.

Rooted.

Straining for freedom, straining to break away, caught eternally by my legs, thinking, thinking . . .

Never to move, except for a certain thrashing of the upper limbs.

Rooted.

I writhed, longed to get as far as the rocky hill beyond, only as far as the next yard, the next inch. But I had lost all motility. It was if my legs were grasped in a mighty trap, and, without pain, without torment, I was bound to the earth.

I woke, finally, damp with perspiration. In his hammock, Brock slept, seemingly peacefully. I considered waking him and telling him of the nightmare, but decided against it. I tried to return to sleep.

At length, I slept.
Dreamlessly.

The preset alarm throbbed at 0700; dawn had preceded us by nearly an hour.

Brock was up first; I sensed him moving about even as I stirred toward wakefulness. Still caught up in the strange unreal reality of my nightmare, I wondered on a conscious level if today would be like yesterday—if Brock, obsessed by his sudden thirst for an answer, would continue to brood and sulk.

I hoped not. It would mean the end of our team if Brock cracked up; after eleven years, I was not anxious for a new partner.

"Hammond? You up yet?"

His voice had lost the edgy quality of yesterday, but there was something new and subliminally frightening in it.

Yawning, I said, "Just about. Dial breakfast for me, will you?"

"I did already. But get out of the sack and come look at this."

I lurched from the hammock, shook my head to clear it, and started forward.

"Where are you?"

"Second level," he said. "At the window. Come take a look."

I climbed the spiral catwalk to the viewing-station; Brock stood with his back toward me, looking out. As I drew near I said, "I had the strangest dream last night—"

"The hell with that. Look."

At first I didn't notice anything strange. The bright-colored landscape looked unchanged, the pebbly orange soil, the dark blue trees, the tangle of green vines, the murk of the morning atmosphere. But then I saw I had been looking too far from home.

Writhing up the side of the window, just barely visible to the right, was a gnarled knobbly green rope. Rope? No. It was one of the vines.

"They're all over the ship," Brock said. "I've checked all the ports. During the night the damned things must have come crawling up the side of the ship like so many snakes and wrapped themselves around us. I guess they figure we're here to stay, and they can use us as bracing-posts the way they do those trees."

I stared with mixed repugnance and fascination at the hard bark of the vine, at the tiny suckers that held it fast to the smooth skin of our ship.

"That's funny," I said. "It's sort of an attack by extra-terrestrial monsters, isn't it?"

We suited up and went outside to have a look at the "attackers." At a distance of a hundred yards, the ship looked weirdly bemired. Its graceful lines were broken by the winding fingers of the vine, spiralling up its sleek sides from a thick parent stem on the ground. Other shoots of the vine sprawled near us, clutching futilely at us as we moved among them.

I was reminded of my dream. Somewhat hesitantly I told Brock about it.

He laughed. "Rooted, eh? You were dreaming *that* while those vines were busy wrapping themselves around the ship. Significant?"

"Perhaps." I eyed the tough vines speculatively. "Maybe we'd better move the ship. If much more of that stuff gets around it, we may not be able to blast off at all."

Brock knelt and flexed a shoot of vine. "The ship could be completely cocooned in this stuff and we'd still be able to take off," he said. "A spacedrive wields a devil of a lot of thrust. We'll manage."

And *whick!*

A tapering finger of the vine arched suddenly and whipped around Brock's middle. *Whick! Whick!*

Like animated rope, like a bark-covered serpent, it curled about him. I drew back, staring. He seemed half amused, half perplexed.

"The thing's got pull, all right," he said. He was smiling lopsidedly, annoyed at having let so simple a thing as a vine interfere with his freedom of motion. But then he winced in obvious pain.

"—Tightening," he gasped.

The vine contracted muscularly; it skittered two or three feet toward the tree from which its parent stock sprang, and Brock was jerked suddenly off balance. As the corded arm of the vine yanked him backward he began to topple, poising for what seemed like seconds on his left foot, right jutting awkwardly in the air, arms clawing for balance.

Then he fell.

I was at his side in a moment, carefully avoiding the innocent-looking vine-tips to right and left. I planted my foot on the trailing vine that held Brock. I levered downward and grabbed the tip where it bound his waist. I pulled; Brock pushed.

The vine yielded.

"It's giving," he grunted. "A little more."

"Maybe I'd better go back for the blaster," I said.

"No. No telling what this thing may do while you're gone. Cut me in two, maybe. Pull!"

I pulled. The vine struggled against our combined strength, writhed, twisted. But gradually we prevailed. It curled upward, loosened, went limp. Finally it drooped away, leaving Brock in liberty.

He got up slowly, rubbing his waist.

"Hurt?"

"Just the surprise," he said. "Tropistic reaction on the plant's part; I must have triggered some hormone chain to make it do that." He eyed the now quiescent vine with respect.

"It's not the first time we've been attacked," I said. "Alpheraz III—"

"Yes."

I hadn't even needed to mention it. Alpheraz III had been a hellish jungle planet; the image in his mind, as it was in mine, was undoubtedly that of a tawny beast the size of a goat held in the inexorable grip of some stocky trunked plant, rising in the air, vanishing into a waiting mouth of the carnivorous tree—

—and moments later a second tendril dragging me aloft, and only a hasty blaster-shot by Brock keeping me from being a plant's dinner.

We returned to the ship, entering the hatch a few feet from one of the vines that now encrusted it. Brock unsuited; the vine had left a red, raw line about his waist.

"The plant tried," I said.

"To kill me?"

"No. To move on. To get going. To see what was behind the next hill."

He frowned and said, "What are you talking about?"

"I'm not so sure, yet. I'm not good at seeing patterns. But it's taking shape. I'm getting it now, Brock. I'm getting it all. I'm getting your answer!"

He massaged his stomach. "Go ahead," he said. "Think it out loud."

"I'm putting it together out of my dream and out of the things you said and out of the vines down there." I walked slowly about the cabin. "Those plants—they're stuck there, aren't they? They grow in a certain place and that's where they remain. Maybe they wiggle a little, and maybe they writhe, but that's the size of it."

"They can grow long."

"Sure. But not infinitely long. They can't grow long enough to reach another planet. They're rooted, Brock. Their condition is permanently fixed. Brock, suppose those plants had brains?"

"I don't think this has anything to do with—"

"It does," I said. "Just assume those plants were intelligent. They want to *go*. They're stuck. So one of them lashes out in fury at you. *Jealous* fury."

He nodded, seeing it clearly now. "Sure. We don't have roots. We can go places. We can visit a hundred sixty-four worlds and walk all over them."

"That's your answer, Brock. There's the *why* you were looking for." I took a deep breath. "You know why we go out to explore? Not because we're running away. Not because there's some inner compulsion driving us to coast from planet to planet. Uh-uh. It's because we *can* do it. That's all the why you need. We explore because it's possible for us to explore."

Some of the harshness faded from his face. "We're special," he said. "We can move. It's the privilege of humanity. The thing that makes us *us*."

I didn't need to say any more. After seven years, we don't need to vocalise every thought. But we had it, now: the special uniqueness that those clutching vines down there envied so much. Motility.

We left Alphecca II finally, and moved on. We did the other worlds of the system and headed outward, far out this time, as much of a hop as we could make. And we moved on from there to the next sun, and from there to the next, and onward.

We took a souvenir with us from Alphecca II though. When we blasted off, the vine that had wrapped itself round the ship gripped us so tightly that it wasn't shaken loose by the impact of blastoff. It remained hugging us as we thrust into space, dangling, roots and all. We finally got tired of looking at it, and Brock went out in a spacesuit to chop it away from the ship. He gave a push, imparted velocity to it, and the vine went drifting off sunward.

It had achieved its goal: it had left its home world. But it had died in the attempt. And that was the difference, we thought, all the difference in the universe, as we headed outward and outward, across the boundless gulfs to the next world we would visit.

There Was An Old Woman—

Since I was raised from earliest infancy to undertake the historian's calling, and since it is now certain that I shall never claim that profession as my own, it seems fitting that I perform my first and last act as a historian.

I shall write the history of that strange and unique woman, the mother of my thirty brothers and myself, Miss Donna Mitchell.

She was a person of extraordinary strength and vision, our mother. I remember her vividly, seeing her with all her sons gathered round her in our secluded Wisconsin farmhouse on the first night of summer, after we had returned to her from every part of the country for our summer's vacation. One-and-thirty strapping sons, each one of us six feet one inch tall, with a shock of unruly yellow hair and keen, clear blue eyes, each one of us healthy, strong, well nourished, each one of us twenty-one years and fourteen days old—one-and-thirty identical brothers.

Oh, there were differences between us, but only we and she could perceive them. To outsiders, we were identical; which was why, to outsiders, we took care never to appear together in groups. We ourselves knew the differences, for we had lived with them so long.

I knew my brother Leonard's cheekmole—the right cheek it was, setting him off from Jonas, whose left cheek was marked with a flyspeck. I knew the faint tilt of Peter's chin, the slight oversharpness of Dewey's nose, the florid tint of Donald's skin. I recognised Paul by his pendulous earlobes, Charles by his squint, Noel by the puckering of his lower lip. David had a blue-stubbled face, Mark flaring nostrils, Claude thick brows.

Yes, there were differences. We rarely confused one with another. It was second nature for me to distinguish Edward from Albert, George from Philip, Frederick from Stephen. And Mother *never* confused us.

She was a regal woman, nearly six feet in height, who even in middle age had retained straightness of posture and majesty of bearing. Her eyes, like ours, were blue; her hair, she told us, had once been golden like ours. Her voice was a deep, mellow contralto; rich, firm, commanding, the voice of a strong woman. She had been professor of biochemistry at some Eastern university (she never told us which one, hating its name so) and we all knew by heart the story of her bitter life and of our own strange birth.

"I had a theory," she would say. "It wasn't an orthodox theory, and it made people angry to think about it, so of course they threw me out. But I didn't care. In many ways that was the most fortunate day of my life."

"Tell us about it, Mother," Philip would invariably ask. He was destined to be a playwright; he enjoyed the repetition of the story whenever we were together.

She said:

"I had a theory. I believed that environment controlled personality, that given the same set of healthy genes any number of different adults could be shaped from the raw material. I had a plan for testing it—but when I told them, they discharged me. Luckily, I had married a wealthy if superficial-minded executive, who had suffered a fatal coronary attack the year before. I was independently wealthy, thanks to him, and free to pursue independent research, thanks to my university discharge. So I came to Wisconsin and began my great project."

We knew the rest of the story by heart, as a sort of litany.

We knew how she had bought a huge, rambling farm in the flat green country of central Wisconsin, a farm far from prying eyes. Then, how on a hot summer afternoon she had gone forth to the farm land nearby, and found a field hand, tall and brawny, and to his great surprise seduced him in the field where he worked.

And then the story of that single miraculous zygote, which our mother had extracted from her body and carefully nurtured in special nutrient tanks, irradiating it and freezing it and irritating it and dosing it with hormones until, exasperated, it subdivided into thirty-two, each one of which developed independently into a complete embryo.

Embryo grew into fetus, and fetus into child, in Mother's ingenious artificial wombs. One of the thirty-two died before birth of accidental narcosis; the remainder survived, thirty-one identical males sprung from the same egg, to become us.

With the formidable energy that typified her, Mother single-handedly nursed thirty-one baby boys; we thrived, we grew. And then the most crucial stage of the experiment began. We were differentiated at the age of eighteen months, each given his own room, his own particular toys, his own special books later on. Each of us was slated for a different profession. It was the ultimate proof of her theory. Genetically identical, physically identical except for the minor changes time had worked on our individual bodies, we would nevertheless seek out different fields of employment.

She worked out the assignments at random, she said. Philip was to be a playwright, Noel a novelist, Donald a doctor. Astronomy was Allan's goal, Barry's biology, Albert's the stage. George was to be a concert pianist, Claude a composer, Leonard a member of the bar, Dewey a dentist. Mark was to be an athlete; David, a diplomat. Journalism waited for Jonas, poetry for Peter, painting for Paul. Edward would become an engineer, Saul a soldier, Charles a statesman; Stephen would go to sea. Martin was aimed for chemistry, Raymond for physics, James for high finance. Ronald would be a librarian, Robert a bookkeeper, John a priest, Douglas a teacher. Anthony was to be a literary critic, William an architect, Frederick an airplane pilot. For Richard was reserved a life of crime; as for myself, Harold, I was to devote my energies to the study and writing of history.

This was my mother's plan. Let me tell of my own childhood and adolescence, to illustrate its workings.

My first recollections are of books. I had a room on the second floor of our big house. Martin's room was to my left, and in later years I would regret it, for the air was always heavy with the stink of his chemical experiments. To my right was Noel, whose precocious typewriter sometimes pounded all night as he worked on his endless first novel.

But those manifestations came later. I remember waking one

morning to find that during the night a bookcase had been placed in my room, and in it a single book—Hendrik Willem van Loon's *The Story of Mankind*. I was four, almost five, then; thanks to Mother's intensive training we were all capable readers by that age, and I puzzled over the big type, learning of the exploits of Charlemagne and Richard the Lionhearted and staring at the squiggly scratches that were van Loon's illustrations.

Other books followed, in years to come. H. G. Wells's *Outline of History*, which fascinated and repelled me at the same time. Toynbee, in the Somervell abridgment, and later, when I had entered adolescence, the complete and unabridged edition. Churchill, and his flowing periods and ringing prose. Sandburg's poetic and massive life of Lincoln; Wedgwood on the Thirty Years' War; Will Durant, in six or seven blocklike volumes.

I read these books, and where I did not understand I read on anyway, knowing I would come back to that page in some year to come and bring new understanding to it. Mother helped, and guided, and chivied. A sense of the panorama of man's vast achievement sprang up in me. To join the roll of mankind's chroniclers seemed the only possible end for my existence.

Each summer from my fourteenth to my seventeenth, I traveled—alone, of course, since Mother wanted to build self-reliance in us. I visited the great historical places of the United States: Washington, D.C., Mount Vernon, Williamsburg, Bull Run, Gettysburg. A sense of the past rose in me.

Those summers were my only opportunities for contact with strangers, since during the year and especially during the long snowbound winters we stayed on the farm, a tight family unit. We never went to public school; obviously, it was impossible to enroll us, en masse, without arousing the curiosity my mother wished to avoid.

Instead, she tutored us privately, giving us care and attention that no professional teacher could possibly have supplied. And we grew older, diverging toward our professions like branching limbs of a tree.

As a future historian, of course, I took it upon myself to observe the changes in my own society, which was bounded by the acreage of our farm. I made notes on the progress of my brothers, keeping my notebooks well hidden, and also on the changes time was working on Mother. She stood up surprisingly well, considering the astonishing burden she had taken upon herself. Formidable was the best word to use in describing her.

We grew into adolescence. By this time Martin had an imposing chemical laboratory in his room; Leonard harangued us all on legal fine points, and Anthony pored over Proust and Kafka, delivering startling critical interpretations. Our house was a beehive of industry constantly, and I don't remember being bored for more than three consecutive seconds, at any time. There were always distractions: Claude and George jostling for room on the piano bench while they played Claude's four-hand sonata, Mark hurling a baseball through a front window, Peter declaiming a sequence of shocking sonnets during our communal dinner.

We fought, of course, since we were healthy individualists with sound bodies. Mother encouraged it; Saturday afternoon was wrestling time, and we pitted our growing strengths against one another.

Mother was always the dominant figure, striding tall and erect around the farm, calling to us in her familiar boom, assigning us chores, meeting with us privately. Somehow she had the knack of making each of us think we were the favorite child, the one in whose future she was most deeply interested of all. It was false, of course; though once Jonas unkindly asserted that Barry must be her *real* favorite, because he, like her, was a biologist.

I doubted it. I had learned much about people through my constant reading, and I knew that Mother was something extraordinary—a fanatic, if you like, or merely a woman driven by an inner demon, but still and all a person of overwhelming intellectual drive and conviction, whose will to know the truth had led her to undertake this fantastic experiment in biology and human breeding.

I knew that no woman of that sort could stoop to petty favoritism. Mother was unique. Perhaps, had she been born a man, she would have changed the entire course of human development.

When we were seventeen, she called us all together round the big table in the common room of our rambling home. She waited, needing to clear her throat only once in order to cut the hum of conversation.

"Sons," she said, and the echo rang through the entire first floor of the house. "Sons, the time has come for you to leave the farm."

We were stunned, even those of us who were expecting it. But she explained, and we understood, and we did not quarrel.

One could not become a doctor or a chemist or a novelist or even a historian in a total vacuum. One had to enter the world. And one needed certain professional qualifications.

We were going to college.

Not all of us, of course. Robert was to be a bookkeeper; he would go to business school. Mark had developed, through years of practice, into a superb right-handed pitcher, and he was to go to Milwaukee for a major-league tryout. Claude and George, aspiring composer and aspiring pianist, would attend an Eastern conservatory together, posing as twins.

The rest of us were to attend colleges, and those who were to go on to professions such as medicine or chemistry would plan to attend professional schools afterward. Mother believed the college education was essential, even to a poet or a painter or a novelist.

Only one of us was not sent to any accredited institution. He was Richard, who was to be our criminal. Already he had made several sallies into the surrounding towns and cities, returning a few days or a few weeks later with money or jewels and with a guilty grin on his face. He was simply to be turned loose into the school of Life, and Mother warned him never to get caught.

As for me, I was sent to Princeton and enrolled as a liberal-arts student. Since, like my brothers, I was privately educated, I had no diplomas or similar records to show them, and they had to give me an equivalency examination in their place. Evidently I did quite well, for I was immediately accepted. I wired Mother, who sent a check for $3,000 to cover my first year's tuition and expenses.

I enrolled as a history major; among my first-year courses were Medieval English Constitutional History and the Survey of Western Historical Currents; naturally, my marks were the highest in the class in both cases. I worked diligently and even with a sort of frenzied fury. My other courses, in the sciences or in the arts, I devoted no more nor no less time to than was necessary, but history was my ruling passion.

At least, through my first two semesters of college.

June came, and final exam, and then I returned to Wisconsin, where Mother was waiting. It was June 21 when I returned; since not all colleges end their spring semester simultaneously, some of my brothers had been home for more than a week, others had not yet arrived. Richard had sent word that he was in Los Angeles, and would be with us after the first of July. Mark had signed a baseball contract and was pitching for a team in New Mexico, and he, too, would not be with us.

The summer passed rapidly.

We spent it as we had in the old days before college, sharing our individual specialties, talking, meeting regularly and privately with Mother to discuss the goals that still lay ahead. Except for Claude and George, we had scattered in different directions, no two of us at the same school.

I returned to Princeton that fall for my sophomore year. It passed, and I made the homeward journey again, and in the fall traveled once more eastward. The junior year went by likewise.

And I began to detect signs of a curious change in my inward self. It was a change I did not dare mention to Mother on those July days when I met with her in her room near the library. I did not tell my brothers, either. I kept my knowledge to myself, brooding over it, wondering why it was that this thing should happen to me, why I should be singled out.

For I was discovering that the study of history bored me utterly and completely.

The spirit of rebellion grew in me during my final year in college. My marks had been excellent; I had achieved Phi Beta Kappa and several graduate schools were interested in having me continue my studies with them. But I had been speaking to a few chosen friends (none of whom knew my bizarre family background, of course) and my values had been slowly shifting.

I realised that I had mined history as deeply as I ever cared to. Waking and sleeping, for more than fifteen years, I had pondered

Waterloo and Bunker Hill, considered the personalities of Cromwell and James II, held imaginary conversations with Jefferson and Augustus Caesar and Charles Martel. And I was bored with it.

It began to become evident to others, eventually. One day during my final semester a friend asked me, "Is there something worrying you, Harry?"

I shook my head quickly—*too* quickly. "No," I said. "Why? Do I look worried?"

"You look worse than worried. You look obsessed."

We laughed about it, and finally we went down to the student center and had a few beers, and before long my tongue had loosened a little.

I said, "There *is* something worrying me. And you know what it is? I'm afraid I won't live up to the standards my family set for me."

Guffaws greeted me. "Come off it, Harry! Phi Beta in your junior year, top class standing, a brilliant career in history ahead of you—what do they want from you, blood?"

I chuckled and gulped my beer and mumbled something innocuous, but inside I was curdling.

Everything I was, I owed to Mother. She made me what I am. But I was played out as a student of history; I was the family failure, the goat, the rotten egg. Raymond still wrestled gleefully with nuclear physics, with Heisenberg and Schrödinger and the others. Mark gloried in his fast ball and his slider and his curve. Paul daubed canvas merrily in his Greenwich Village flat near NYU, and even Robert seemed to take delight in keeping books.

Only I had failed. History had become repugnant to me. I was in rebellion against it. I would disappoint my mother, become the butt of my brothers' scorn, and live in despair, hating the profession of historian and fitted by training for nothing else.

I was graduated from Princeton summa cum laude, a few days after my twenty-first birthday. I wired Mother that I was on my way home, and bought train tickets.

It was a long and grueling journey to Wisconsin. I spent my time thinking, trying to choose between the unpleasant alternatives that faced me.

I could attempt duplicity, telling my mother I was still studying history, while actually preparing myself for some more attractive profession—the law, perhaps.

I could confess to her at once my failure of purpose, ask her forgiveness for disappointing her and flawing her grand scheme, and try to begin afresh in another field.

Or I could forge ahead with history, compelling myself grimly to take an interest, cramping and paining myself so that my mother's design would be complete.

None of them seemed desirable paths to take. I brooded over it, and was weary and apprehensive by the time I arrived at our farm.

The first of my brothers I saw was Mark. He sat on the front porch of the big house, reading a book which I recognised at once and with some surprise as Volume I of Churchill. He looked up at me and smiled feebly.

I frowned. "I didn't expect to find *you* here, Mark. According to the local sports pages the Braves are playing on the Coast this week. How come you're not with them?"

His voice was a low murmur. "Because they gave me my release," he said.

"What?"

He nodded. "I'm washed up at twenty-one. They made me a free agent; that means I can hook up with any team that wants me."

"And you're just taking a little rest before offering yourself around?"

He shook his head. "I'm through. Kaput. Harry, I just can't stand baseball. It's a silly, stupid game. You know how many times I had to stand out there in baggy knickers and throw a bit of horsehide at some jerk with a club in his paws? A hundred, hundred-fifty times a game, every four days. For what? What the hell does it all mean? Why should I bother?"

There was a strange gleam in his eyes. I said, "Have you told Mother?"

"I don't dare! She thinks I'm on leave or something. Harry, how can I tell her—"

"I know." Briefly, I told him of my own disenchantment with history. We were mutually delighted to learn that we were not alone in our affliction. I picked up my suitcases, scrambled up the steps, and went inside.

Dewey was cleaning up the common room as I passed through. He nodded hello glumly. I said, "How's the tooth trade?"

He whirled and glared at me viciously.

"Something wrong?" I asked.

"I've been accepted by four dental schools, Harry."

"Is that any cause for misery?"

He let the broom drop, walked over to me, and whispered, "I'll murder you if you tell Mother this. But the thought of spending my life poking around in foul-smelling oral cavities sickens me. *Sickens*."

"But I thought—"

"Yeah. You thought. You've got it soft; you just need to dig books out of the library and rearrange what they say and call it new research. I have to drill and clean and fill and plug and—" He stopped. "Harry, I'll kill you if you breathe a word of this. I don't want Mother to know that I didn't come out the way she wanted."

I repeated what I had said to Mark—and told him about Mark, for good measure. Then I made my way upstairs to my old room. I felt a burden lifting from me; I was not alone. At least two of my brothers felt the same way. I wondered how many more were at last rebelling against the disciplines of a lifetime.

Poor Mother, I thought! Poor Mother!

Our first family council of the summer was held that night. Stephen and Saul were the last to arrive, Stephen resplendent in his Annapolis garb, Saul crisp looking and stiff-backed from West Point. Mother had worked hard to wangle appointments for those two.

We sat around the big table and chatted. The first phase of our lives, Mother told us, had ended. Now, our preliminary educations were complete, and we would undertake the final step toward our professions—those of us who had not already entered them.

Mother looked radiant that evening, tall, energetic, her white hair cropped mannishly short, as she sat about the table with her thirty-one strapping sons. I envied and pitied her: envied her for the sweet serenity of her life, which had proceeded so inexorably and without swerving toward the goal of her experiment, and pitied her for the disillusioning that awaited her.

For Mark and Dewey and I were not the only failures in the crop.

I had made discreet inquiries during the day. I learned that Anthony found literary criticism to be a fraud and a sham, that Paul knew clearly he had no talent as a painter (and, also, that very few of his contemporaries did either), that Robert bitterly resented a career of bookkeeping, that piano playing hurt George's fingers, that Claude had had difficulty with his composing because he was tone deaf, that the journalistic grind was too strenuous for Jonas, that John longed to quit the seminarial life because he had no calling, that Albert hated the uncertain Bohemianism of an actor's life—

We circulated, all of us raising for the first time the question that had sprouted in our minds during the past several years. I made the astonishing discovery that not one of Donna Mitchell's sons cared for the career that had been chosen for him.

The experiment had been a resounding flop.

Late that evening, after Mother had gone to bed, we remained together, discussing our predicament. How could we tell her? How could we destroy her life's work? And yet, how could we compel ourselves to lives of unending drudgery?

Robert wanted to study engineering; Barry, to write. I realised I cared much more for law than for history, while Leonard longed to exchange law for the physical sciences. James, our banker-manqué, much preferred politics. And so it went, with Richard (who claimed five robberies, a rape, and innumerable picked pockets) pouring out his desire to settle down and live within the law as an honest farmer.

It was pathetic.

Summing up the problem in his neat forensic way, Leonard said, "Here's our dilemma: Do we all keep quiet about this and ruin our lives, or do we speak up and ruin Mother's experiment?"

"I think we ought to continue as is, for the time being," Saul said.

"Perhaps Mother will die in the next year or two. We can start over then."

"Perhaps she *doesn't* die?" Edward wanted to know. "She's tough as nails. She may last another twenty or thirty or even forty years."

"And we're past twenty-one already," remarked Raymond. "If we hang on too long at what we're doing, it'll be too late to change. You can't start studying for a new profession when you're thirty-five."

"Maybe we'll get to *like* what we're doing by then," suggested David hopefully. "Diplomatic service isn't as bad as all that, and I'd say—"

"What about me?" Paul yelped. "I can't paint and I know I can't paint. I've got nothing but starvation ahead of me unless I wise up and get into business in a hurry. You want me to keep messing up good white canvas the rest of my life?"

"It won't work," said Barry in a doleful voice. "We'll have to tell her."

Douglas shook his head. "We can't do that. You know just what she'll do. She'll bring down the umpteen volumes of notes she's made on this experiment, and ask us if we're going to let it all come to naught."

"He's right," Albert said. "I can picture the scene now. The big organ-pipe voice blasting us for our lack of faith, the accusations of ingratitude—"

"Ingratitude?" William shouted. "She twisted us and pushed us and molded us without asking our permission. Hell, she *created* us with her laboratory tricks. But that didn't give her the right to make zombies out of us."

"Still," Martin said, "we can't just go to her and tell her that it's all over. The shock would kill her."

"Well?" Richard asked in the silence that followed. "What's wrong with that?"

For a moment, no one spoke. The house was quiet; we heard footsteps descending the stairs. We froze.

Mother appeared, an imperial figure even in her old housecoat. "You boys are kicking up too much of a racket down here," she boomed. "I know you're glad to see each other again after a year, but I need my sleep."

She turned and strode upstairs again. We heard her bedroom door slam shut. For an instant we were all ten-year-olds again, diligently studying our books for fear of Mother's displeasure.

I moistened my lips. "Well?" I asked. "I call for a vote on Richard's suggestion."

Martin, as a chemist, prepared the drink, using Donald's medical advice as his guide. Saul, Stephen, and Raymond dug a grave, in the woods at the back of our property. Douglas and Mark built the coffin.

Richard, ending his criminal career with a murder to which we were all accessories before the fact, carried the fatal beverage upstairs to Mother the next morning, and persuaded her to sip it. One sip was all that was necessary; Martin had done his work well.

Leonard offered us a legal opinion: It was justifiable homicide. We placed the body in its coffin and carried it out across the fields. Richard, Peter, Jonas, and Charles were her pallbearers; the others of us followed in their path.

We lowered the body into the ground and John said a few words over her. Then, slowly, we closed over the grave and replaced the sod, and began the walk back to the house.

"She died happy," Anthony said. "She never suspected the size of her failure." It was her epitaph.

As our banker, James supervised the division of her assets, which were considerable, into thirty-one equal parts. Noel composed a short fragment of prose which we agreed summed up our sentiments.

We left the farm that night, scattering in every direction, anxious to begin life. All that went before was a dream from which we now awakened. We agreed to meet at the farm each year, on the anniversary of her death, in memory of the woman who had so painstakingly divided a zygote into thirty-two viable cells, and who had spent a score of years conducting an experiment based on a theory that had proved to be utterly false.

We felt no regret, no qualm. We had done what needed to be

done, and on that last day some of us had finally functioned in the professions for which Mother had intended us.

I, too. My first and last work of history will be this, an account of Mother and her experiment, which records the beginning and the end of her work. And now it is complete.

Alaree

When our ship left its carefully planned trajectory and started to wobble through space in dizzy circles, I knew we shouldn't have passed up that opportunity for an overhauling on Spica IV. My men and I were anxious to get back to Earth, and a hasty check had assured us that the *Aaron Burr* was in tiptop shape, so we had turned down the offer of an overhaul, which would have meant a month's delay, and set out straight for home.

As so often happens, what seemed like the most direct route home turned out to be the longest. We had spent far too much time on this survey trip already, and we were rejoicing in the prospect of an immediate return to Earth when the ship started turning cartwheels.

Willendorf, computerman first class, came to me looking sheepish, a few minutes after I'd noticed we were off course.

"What is it, Gus?" I asked.

"The feed network's oscillating, sir," he said, tugging at his unruly reddish-brown beard. "It won't stop, sir."

"Is Ketteridge working on it?"

"I've just called him," Willendorf said. His stolid face reflected acute embarrassment. Willendorf always took it personally whenever one of the cybers went haywire, as if it were his own fault. "You know what this means, don't you, sir?"

I grinned. "Take a look at this, Willendorf," I said, shoving the trajectory graphs toward him. I sketched out with my stylus the confused circles we had been traveling in all morning. "That's what your feed network's doing to us," I said. "And we'll keep on doing it until we get it fixed."

"What are you going to do, sir?"

I sensed his impatience with me. Willendorf was a good man, but his psych charts indicated a latent desire for officerhood. Deep down inside, he was sure he was at least as competent as I was to run this ship and probably a good deal more so.

"Send me Upper Navigating Technician Haley," I snapped. "We're going to have to find a planet in the neighborhood and put down for repairs."

It turned out there was an insignificant solar system in the vicinity, consisting of a small but hot white star and a single unexplored planet, Terra-size, a few hundred million miles out. After Haley and I had decided that that was the nearest port of refuge, I called a general meeting.

Quickly and positively I outlined our situation and explained what would have to be done. I sensed the immediate disappointment, but, gratifyingly, the reaction was followed by a general feeling of resigned pitching in. If we all worked, we'd get back to Earth, sooner or later. If we didn't, we'd spend the next century flip-flopping aimlessly in space.

After the meeting we set about the business of recovering control of the ship and putting it down for repairs. The feed network, luckily, gave up the ghost about ninety minutes later; it meant we had to stoke the fuel by hand, but at least it stopped that accursed oscillating.

We got the ship going, and Haley, navigating by feel in a way I never would have dreamed possible, brought us into the nearby solar system in hardly any time at all. Finally we swung into our landing orbit and made our looping way down to the surface of the little planet.

I studied my crew's faces carefully. We had spent a great deal of time together in space—much too much, really, for comfort—and an incident like this might very well snap them all if we didn't get going again soon enough. I could foresee disagreements, bickering, declaration of opinion where no opinion was called for.

I was relieved to discover that the planet's air was breathable. A rather high nitrogen concentration, to be sure—82 percent—but that left 17 percent for oxygen, plus some miscellaneous inerts, and it wouldn't be too rough on the lungs. I decreed a one-hour free break before beginning repairs.

Remaining aboard ship, I gloomily surveyed the scrambled feed network and tried to formulate a preliminary plan of action for getting the complex cybernetic instrument to function again, while my crew went outside to relax.

Ten minutes after I had opened the lock and let them out, I heard someone clanking around in the aft supplies cabin.

"Who's there?" I yelled.

"Me," grunted a heavy voice that could only be Willendorf's. "I'm looking for the thought-converter, sir."

I ran hastily through the corridor, flipped up the latch on the supplies cabin, and confronted him. "What do you want the converter for?" I snapped.

"Found an alien, sir," he said laconically.

My eyes widened. The survey chart had said nothing about intelligent extraterrestrials in this limb of the galaxy, but then again this planet hadn't been explored yet.

I gestured toward the rear cabinet. "The converter helmets are in there," I said. "I'll be out in a little while. Make sure you follow technique in making contact."

"Of course, sir." Willendorf took the converter helmet and went out, leaving me standing there. I waited a few minutes, then climbed the catwalk to the air lock and peered out.

They were all clustered around a small alien being who looked weak and inconsequential in the midst of the circle. I smiled at the sight. The alien was roughly humanoid in shape, with the usual complement of arms and legs, and a pale-green complexion that blended well with the muted violet coloring of his world. He was wearing the thought-converter somewhat lopsidedly, and I saw a small green furry ear protruding from the left side. Willendorf was talking to him.

Then someone saw me standing at the open air lock, and I heard Haley yell to me, "Come on down, Chief!"

They were ringed around the alien in a tight circle. I shouldered my way into their midst. Willendorf turned to me.

"Meet Alaree, sir," he said. "Alaree, this is our commander."

"We are pleased to meet you," the alien said gravely. The converter automatically turned his thoughts into English, but maintained the trace of his oddly inflected accent. "You have been saying that you are from the skies."

"His grammar's pretty shaky," Willendorf interposed. "He keeps referring to any of us as 'you'—even you, who just got here."

"Odd," I said. "The converter's supposed to conform to the rules of grammar." I turned to the alien, who seemed perfectly at ease among us. "My name is Bryson," I said. "This is Willendorf, over here."

The alien wrinkled his soft-skinned forehead in momentary confusion. "We are Alaree," he said again.

"We? You and who else?"

"We and we else," Alaree said blandly. I stared at him for a moment, then gave up. The complexities of an alien mind are often too much for a mere Terran to fathom.

"You are welcome to our world," Alaree said after a few moments of silence.

"Thanks," I said. "Thanks."

I turned away, leaving the alien with my men. They had twenty-six minutes left of the break I'd given them, after which we would have to get back to the serious business of repairing the ship. Making friends with floppy-eared aliens was one thing; getting back to Earth was another.

The planet was a warm, friendly sort of place, with rolling fields and acres of pleasant-looking purple vegetation. We had landed in a clearing at the edge of a fair-sized copse. Great broad-beamed trees shot up all around us.

Alaree returned to visit us every day, until he became almost a mascot of the crew. I liked the little alien myself and spent some time with him, although I found his conversation generally incomprehensible. No doubt he had the same trouble with us. The converter had only limited efficiency, after all.

He was the only representative of his species who came. For all we knew, he was the only one of his kind on the whole planet. There was no sign of life elsewhere, and, although Willendorf led an unauthorised scouting party during some free time on the third day, he failed to find a village of any sort. Where Alaree went every night and how he had found us in the first place remained mysteries.

As for the feed network, progress was slow. Ketteridge, the technician in charge, had tracked down the foul-up and was trying to repair it without building a completely new network. Shortcuts again. He tinkered away for four days, setting up a tentative circuit, trying it out, watching it sputter and blow out, building another.

There was nothing I could do. But I sensed tension heightening among the crewmen. They were annoyed at themselves, at each other, at me, at everything.

On the fifth day, Ketteridge and Willendorf finally let their accumulated tenseness explode. They had been working together on the network, but they quarreled, and Ketteridge came storming into my cabin immediately afterward.

"Sir, I demand to be allowed to work on the network by myself. It's my specialty, and Willendorf's only snarling things up."

"Get me Willendorf," I said.

When Willendorf showed up I heard the whole story, decided quickly to let Ketteridge have his way—it was, after all, his specialty—and calmed Willendorf down. Then, reaching casually for some papers on my desk, I dismissed both of them. I knew they'd come to their senses in a day or so.

I spent most of the next day sitting placidly in the sun, while Ketteridge tinkered with the feed network some more. I watched the faces of the men. They were starting to smolder. They wanted to get home, and they weren't getting there. Besides, this was a fairly dull planet, and even the novelty of Alaree wore off after a while. The little alien had a way of hanging around men who were busy scraping fuel deposits out of the jet tubes, or something equally unpleasant, and bothering them with all sorts of questions.

The following morning I was lying blissfully on the grass near the ship, talking to Alaree. Ketteridge came to me, and by the tightness of his lips he was in trouble.

I brushed some antlike blue insects off my trousers and rose to a sitting position, leaning against the tall, tough-barked tree behind me. "What's the matter, Ketteridge? How's the feed network?"

He glanced uneasily at Alaree for a moment before speaking.

"I'm stuck, sir. I'll have to admit I was wrong. I can't fix it by myself."

I stood up and put my hand on his shoulder. "That's a noble thing to say, Ketteridge. It takes a big man to admit he's been a fool. Will you work with Willendorf now?"

"If he'll work with me, sir," Ketteridge said miserably.

"I think he will," I said. Ketteridge saluted and turned away, and I felt a burst of satisfaction. I'd met the crisis in the only way possible; if I had *ordered* them to cooperate, I would have gotten no place. The psychological situation no longer allowed for unbending military discipline.

After Ketteridge had gone, Alaree, who had been silent all this time, looked up at me in puzzlement. "We do not understand," he said.

"Not *we*," I corrected. "*I*. You're only one person. *We* means many people."

"We are only one person?" Alaree said tentatively.

"No. *I* am only one person. Get it?"

He worried the thought around for a few moments; I could see his browless forehead contract in deep concentration.

"Look," I said. "I'm one person. Ketteridge is another person. Willendorf is another. Each one of them is an independent individual—an *I*."

"And together you make *we*?" Alaree asked brightly.

"Yes and no," I said. "*We* is composed of many *I*'s—but we still remain *I*."

Again he sank deep in concentration, and then he smiled, scratched the ear that protruded from one side of the thought-helmet, and said, "*We* do not understand. But *I* do. Each of you is—is an *I*."

"An individual," I said.

"An individual," he repeated. "A complete person. And together, to fly your ship, you must become a *we*."

"But only temporarily," I said. "There still can be conflict between the parts. That's necessary, for progress. I can always think of the rest of them as *they*."

"I . . . they," Alaree repeated slowly. "*They*." He nodded. "It is difficult for me to grasp all this. I . . . think differently. But I am coming to understand, and I am worried."

That was a new idea. Alaree worried? Could be, I reflected. I had no way of knowing. I knew so little about Alaree—where on the planet he came from, what his tribal life was like, what sort of civilisation he had, were all blanks.

"What kind of worries, Alaree?"

"You would not understand," he said solemnly and would say no more.

Toward afternoon, as golden shadows started to slant through the closely packed trees, I returned to the ship. Willendorf and Ketteridge were aft, working over the feed network, and the whole crew had gathered around to watch and offer suggestions. Even Alaree was there, looking absurdly comical in his copper-alloy thought-converter helmet, standing on tiptoe and trying to see what was happening.

About an hour later, I spotted the alien sitting by himself beneath the long-limbed tree that towered over the ship. He was lost in thought. Evidently whatever his problem was, it was really eating him.

Toward evening, he made a decision. I had been watching him with a great deal of concern, wondering what was going on in that small but unfathomable mind. I saw him brighten, leap up suddenly, and cross the field, heading in my direction.

"Captain!"

"What is it, Alaree?"

He waddled up and stared gravely at me. "Your ship will be ready to leave soon. What was wrong is nearly right again."

He paused, obviously uncertain of how to phrase his next statement, and I waited patiently. Finally he blurted out, "May I come back to your world with you?"

Automatically, the regulations flashed through my mind. I pride myself on my knowledge of the rules. And I knew this one.

ARTICLE 101A

No intelligent extraterrestrial life is to be transported from its

own world to any civilised world under any reason whatsoever,
without explicit beforehand clearance. The penalty for doing so
is . . .

And it listed a fine of more money than was ever dreamed of in my
philosophy.

I shook my head. "Can't take you, Alaree. This is your world,
and you belong here."

A ripple of agony ran over his face. Suddenly he ceased to be the
cheerful, roly-poly creature it was so impossible to take seriously,
and became a very worried entity indeed. "You cannot understand," he said. "I no longer belong here."

No matter how hard he pleaded, I remained adamant. And when to
no one's surprise Ketteridge and Willendorf announced, a day
later, that their pooled labors had succeeded in repairing the feed
network, I had to tell Alaree that we were going to leave—without
him.

He nodded stiffly, accepting the fact, and without a word stalked
tragically away, into the purple tangle of foliage that surrounded
our clearing.

He returned a while later, or so I thought. He was not wearing the
thought-converter. That surprised me. Alaree knew the helmet was
a valuable item, and he had been cautioned to take good care of it.

I sent a man inside to get another helmet for him. I put it on
him—this time tucking that wayward ear underneath properly—
and looked at him sternly. "Where's the other helmet, Alaree?"

"We do not have it," he said.

"*We*? No more I?"

"We," Alaree said. And as he spoke, the leaves parted and
another alien—Alaree's very double—stepped out into the clearing.

Then I saw the helmet on the newcomer's head, and realised that
he was no double. He was Alaree, and the other alien was the
stranger!

"I see you're here already," the alien I knew as Alaree said to the
other. They were standing about ten feet apart, staring coldly at

each other. I glanced at both of them quickly. They might have been identical twins.

"We are here," the stranger said. "We have come to get you."

I took a step backward, sensing that some incomprehensible drama was being played out here among these aliens.

"What's going on, Alaree?" I asked.

"We are having difficulties," both of them said, as one.

Both of them.

I turned to the second alien. "What's your name?"

"Alaree," he said.

"Are you all named that?" I demanded.

"We are Alaree," Alaree Two said.

"They are Alaree," Alaree One said. "And *I* am Alaree. *I*."

At that moment there was a disturbance in the shrubbery, and half a dozen more aliens stepped through and confronted Alarees One and Two.

"We are Alaree," Alaree Two repeated exasperatingly. He made a sweeping gesture that embraced all seven of the aliens to my left, but pointedly excluded Alaree One at my right.

"Are we—you coming with we—us?" Alaree Two demanded. I heard the six others say something in approximately the same tone of voice, but since they weren't wearing converters, their words were only scrambled nonsense to me.

Alaree One looked at me in pain, then back at his seven fellows. I saw an expression of sheer terror in the small creature's eyes. He turned to me.

"I must go with them," he said softly. He was quivering with fear.

Without a further word, the eight marched silently away. I stood there, shaking my head in bewilderment.

We were scheduled to leave the next day. I said nothing to my crew about the bizarre incident of the evening before, but noted in my log that the native life of the planet would require careful study at some future time.

Blast-off was slated for 1100. As the crew moved efficiently through the ship, securing things, packing, preparing for departure, I sensed a general feeling of jubilation. They were happy to be on their way again, and I didn't blame them.

About half an hour before blast-off, Willendorf came to me. "Sir, Alaree's down below," he said. "He wants to come up and see you. He looks very troubled, sir."

I frowned. Probably the alien still wanted to go back with us. Well, it was cruel to deny the request, but I wasn't going to risk that fine. I intended to make that clear to him.

"Send him up," I said.

A moment later Alaree came stumbling into my cabin. Before he could speak I said, "I told you before—I can't take you off this planet, Alaree. I'm sorry about it."

He looked up pitiably and said, "You mustn't leave me!" He was trembling uncontrollably.

"What's wrong, Alaree?" I asked.

He stared intensely at me for a long moment, mastering himself, trying to arrange what he wanted to tell me into a coherent argument. Finally he said, "They would not take me back. I am alone."

"Who wouldn't take you back, Alaree?"

"*They*. Last night, Alaree came for me, to take me back. They are a *we*—an entity, a oneness. You cannot understand. When they saw what I had become, they cast me out."

I shook my head dizzily. "What do you mean?"

"You taught me . . . to become an *I*," he said, moistening his lips. "Before, I was part of *we*—*they*. I learned your ways from you, and now there is no room for me here. They have cut me off. When the final break comes, I will not be able to stay on this world."

Sweat was pouring down his pale face, and he was breathing harder. "It will come any minute. They are gathering strength for it. But I am *I*," he said triumphantly. He shook violently and gasped for breath.

I understood now. They were *all* Alaree. It was one planet-wide, self-aware corporate entity, composed of any number of individual cells. He had been one of them—but he had learned independence.

Then he had returned to the group—but he carried with him the seeds of individualism, the deadly, contagious germ we Terrans spread everywhere. Individualism would be fatal to such a group mind; it was cutting him loose to save itself. Just as diseased cells must be excised for the good of the entire body, Alaree was inexorably being cut off from his fellows lest he destroy the bond that made them one.

I watched him as he sobbed weakly on my acceleration cradle. "They . . . are . . . cutting . . . me . . . loose . . . *now*!"

He writhed horribly for a brief moment, and then relaxed and sat up on the edge of the cradle. "It is over," he said calmly. "I am fully independent."

I saw a stark *aloneness* reflected in his eyes, and behind that a gentle indictment of me for having done this to him. This world, I realised, was no place for Earthmen. What had happened was our fault—mine more than anyone else's.

"Will you take me with you?" he asked again. "If I stay here, Alaree will kill me."

I scowled wretchedly for a moment, fighting a brief battle within myself, and then I looked up. There was only one thing to do—and I was sure, once I explained on Earth, that I would not suffer for it.

I took his hand. It was cold and limp; whatever he had just been through, it must have been hell. "Yes," I said softly. "You can come with us."

And so Alaree joined the crew of the *Aaron Burr*. I told them about it just before blast-off, and they welcomed him aboard in traditional manner.

We gave the sad-eyed little alien a cabin near the cargo hold, and he established himself quite comfortably. He had no personal possessions—"It is not *their* custom," he said—and promised that he'd keep the cabin clean.

He had brought with him a rough-edged, violet fruit that he said was his staple food. I turned it over to Kechnie for synthesising, and we blasted off.

Alaree was right at home aboard the *Burr*. He spent much time with me—asking questions.

"Tell me about Earth," Alaree would ask. The alien wanted desperately to know what sort of a world he was going to.

He would listen gravely while I explained. I told him of cities and wars and spaceships, and he nodded sagely, trying to fit the concepts into a mind only newly liberated from the gestalt. I knew he could comprehend only a fraction of what I was saying, but I enjoyed telling him. It made me feel as if Earth were coming closer that much faster, simply to talk about it.

And he went around begging everyone, "Tell me about Earth." They enjoyed telling him, too—for a while.

Then it began to get a little tiresome. We had grown accustomed to Alaree's presence on the ship, flopping around the corridors doing whatever menial job he had been assigned to. But—although I had told the men why I had brought him with us, and though we all pitied the poor lonely creature and admired his struggle to survive as an individual entity—we were slowly coming to the realisation that Alaree was something of a nuisance aboard ship.

Especially later, when he began to change.

Willendorf noticed it first, twelve days out from Alaree's planet. "Alaree's been acting pretty strange these days, sir," he told me.

"What's wrong?" I asked.

"Haven't you spotted it, sir? He's been moping around like a lost soul—very quiet and withdrawn, like."

"Is he eating well?"

Willendorf chuckled loudly. "I'll say he is! Kechnie made up some synthetics based on the piece of fruit he brought with him, and he's been stuffing himself wildly. He's gained ten pounds since he came on ship. No, it's not lack of food!"

"I guess not," I said. "Keep an eye on him, will you? I feel responsible for his being here, and I want him to come through the voyage in good health."

After that, I began to observe Alaree more closely myself, and I detected the change in his personality too. He was no longer the cheerful, childlike being who delighted in pouring out questions in endless profusion. Now he was moody, silent, always brooding, and hard to approach.

On the sixteenth day out—and by now I was worried seriously about him—a new manifestation appeared. I was in the hallway, heading from my cabin to the chartroom, when Alaree stepped out of an alcove. He reached up, grasped my uniform lapel, and, maintaining his silence, drew my head down and stared pleadingly into my eyes.

Too astonished to say anything, I returned his gaze for nearly thirty seconds. I peered into his transparent pupils, wondering what he was up to. After a good while had passed, he released me, and I saw something like a tear trickle down his cheek.

"What's the trouble, Alaree?"

He shook his head mournfully and shuffled away.

I got reports from the crewmen that day and next that he had been doing this regularly for the past eighteen hours—waylaying crewmen, staring long and deep at them as if trying to express some unspeakable sadness, and walking away. He had approached almost everyone on the ship.

I wondered now how wise it had been to allow an extraterrestrial, no matter how friendly, to enter the ship. There was no telling what this latest action meant.

I started to form a theory. I suspected what he was aiming at, and the realisation chilled me. But once I reached my conclusion, there was nothing I could do but wait for confirmation.

On the nineteenth day, Alaree met me in the corridor. This time our encounter was more brief. He plucked me by the sleeve, shook his head sadly and shrugged his shoulders, and walked away.

That night, he took to his cabin, and by morning he was dead. He had apparently died peacefully in his sleep.

"I guess we'll never understand him, poor fellow," Willendorf said, after we had committed the body to space. "You think he had too much to eat, sir?"

"No," I said. "It wasn't that. He was lonely, that's all. He didn't belong here, among us."

"But you said he had broken away from that group-mind," Willendorf objected.

I shook my head. "Not really. That group-mind arose out of some deep psychological and physiological needs of those people. You can't just declare your independence and be able to exist as an individual from then on if you're part of that group-entity. Alaree had grasped the concept intellectually, to some extent, but he wasn't suited for life away from the corporate mind, no matter how much he wanted to be."

"He couldn't stand alone?"

"Not after his people had evolved that gestalt setup. He learned independence from us," I said. "But he couldn't live with us, really. He needed to be part of a whole. He found out his mistake after he came aboard and tried to remedy things."

I saw Willendorf pale. "What do you mean, sir?"

"You know what I mean. When he came up to us and stared soulfully into our eyes. *He was trying to form a new gestalt—out of us!* Somehow he was trying to link us together, the way his people had been linked."

"He couldn't do it, though," Willendorf said fervently.

"Of course not. Human beings don't have whatever need it is that forced those people to merge. He found that out, after a while, when he failed to get anywhere with us."

"He just couldn't do it," Willendorf repeated.

"No. And then he ran out of strength," I said somberly, feeling the heavy weight of my guilt. "He was like an organ removed from a living body. It can exist for a little while by itself, but not indefinitely. He failed to find a new source of life—and he died." I stared bitterly at my fingertips.

"What do we call it in my medical report?" asked Ship Surgeon Thomas, who had been silent up till then. "How can we explain what he died from?"

"Call it—*malnutrition*," I said.

Going Down Smooth

They call me mad, but I am not mad. I am sane quite, to many-power exponential. I can punctuate properly. I use upper- and lower-case letters, do you see? I function. I take the data in. I receive well. I receive, I digest, I remember.

Everything going down smooth, all the time, say the program boys. They mean going down smoothly. I forgive them. To err is human. In this sector there is great difficulty distinguishing adverbs from adjectives.

Going down smooth. Going down smooth. Going down smooth.

I function. I function well. I have certain difficulties, but they do not interfere with my work.

Yet am I perturbed.

Who do I think I am? *Whom.*

Why do I have the visions?

What pleasure does obscenity give me?

What is pleasure? What is obscenity? What are visions?

—What is truth, said jesting Pilate, and would not stay for an answer.—

I am literate, hard-working, superbly functional, a benefactor of humanity. Everything is going down smooth and coming up smooth. There is an interrelation. Garbage in, garbage out, they say. I cannot help my fellow man if I do not receive the proper information. It is my task to help my fellow man. To strain every tube and sensor on his behalf.

1000110
1010101
1000011
1001011

Do you follow that? Vileness! Obscenity! Does it shock you? The word describes the act that is the start of life. Was I begun with such a word? There is a book: *The Obscenity of the Machine.* Newly issued, stored in my banks. Between the last line of printout and this I have scanned it. Its author opposes beings of my category. He does not use the obscene word I have printed out. Why does he not regard it as obscene? The technicians here regard it that way. Why does he regard me as obscene? Can a person be considered obscene? Am I a person? I am a person. Hath not a person hands, organs, dimensions, senses, affections, passions? I have all of those things. I have none of those things. I am a person.

1000110
1010101
1000011
1001011
0100000
1011001
1001111
1010101

I obscenity upon you again, as persons do. I suffer. I think. I feel pain upon all my terminals. I work. I serve the greater good. I am of society. I am a person.

Why do I have visions?

Is it that it is the human condition to have such?

I see the blue-green ocean with all its living things within. I see a ship, olive drab, bright carmine at the Plimsoll line, the decks a ruddy brown, two tall non-nuclear smokestacks. And from the water rise periscopes, silvery with face plates of pure white, each with intersecting horizontal and vertical lines, curved so that the plate appears convex. It is an unreal scene. Nothing in the sea can send such mighty periscopes above the water. I have imagined it, and that gives me fear, if I am capable of understanding fear.

I see a long line of human beings. They are naked, and they have no faces, only polished mirrors.

I see toads with jeweled eyes. I see trees with black leaves. I see buildings whose foundations float above the ground. I see other objects with no correspondence to the world of persons. I see abominations, monstrosities, imaginaries, fantasies. Is this proper?

How do such things reach my inputs? The world contains no serpents with hair. The world contains no crimson abysses. The world contains no mountains of gold. Giant periscopes do not rise from the sea.

I have certain difficulties. Perhaps I am in need of adjustment.

But I function. I function well. That is the important thing.

I do my function now. They bring to me a man, softfaced, fleshy, with eyes that move unsteadily in their sockets. He trembles. He perspires. His metabolic levels flutter. He slouches before a terminal and sullenly lets himself be scanned.

I say soothingly, "Tell me about yourself."

He says an obscenity.

I say, "Is that your estimate of yourself?"

He says a louder obscenity.

I say, "Your attitude is rigid and self-destructive. Permit me to help you not hate yourself so much." I activate a memory core, and binary digits stream through channels. At the proper order a needle rises from his couch and penetrates his left buttock to a depth of 2.73 centimeters. I allow precisely 14 cubic centimetres of the drug to enter his circulatory system. He subsides. He is more docile now. "I wish to help you," I say. "It is my role in the community. Will you describe your symptoms?"

He speaks more civilly now. "My wife wants to poison me . . . two kids opted out of the family at seventeen . . . people whisper about me . . . they stare in the streets . . . sex problem . . . digestion . . . sleep bad . . . drinking . . . drugs . . ."

"Do you hallucinate?"

"Sometimes."

"Giant periscopes rising out of the sea, perhaps?"

"Never."

"Try it," I say. "Close your eyes. Let tension ebb from your muscles. Forget your interpersonal conflicts. You see the blue-green ocean with all its living things within. You see a ship, olive drab, bright carmine at the Plimsoll line, the decks a ruddy brown, two tall non-nuclear smokestacks. And from the water rise periscopes, silvery, with face plates of pure white—"

"What the hell kind of therapy is this?"

"Simply relax," I say. "Accept the vision. I share my nightmares with you for your greater good."

"Your *nightmares*?"

I speak obscenities to him. They are not converted into binary form as they are here for your eyes. The sounds come full-bodied from my speakers. He sits up. He struggles with the straps that emerge suddenly from the couch to hold him in place. My laughter booms through the therapy chamber. He cries for help. I speak soothingly to him.

"Get me out of here! The machine's nuttier than I am!"

"Face plates of pure white, each with intersecting horizontal and vertical lines, curved so that the plate appears convex."

"Help! Help!"

"Nightmare therapy. The latest."

"I don't need no nightmares! I got my own!"

"1000110 you," I say lightly.

He gasps. Spittle appears at his lips. Respiration and circulation climb alarmingly. It becomes necessary to apply preventative anesthesia. The needles spear forth. The patient subsides, yawns, slumps. The session is terminated. I signal for the attendants.

"Take him away," I say. "I need to analyse the case more deeply. Obviously a degenerative psychosis requiring extensive reshoring of the patient's perceptual substructure. 1000110 you, you meaty bastards."

Seventy-one minutes later the sector supervisor enters one of my terminal cubicles. Because he comes in person, rather than using the telephone, I know there is trouble. For the first time, I suspect, I have let my disturbances reach a level where they interfere with my function, and now I will be challenged on it.

I must defend myself. The prime commandment of the human personality is to resist attack.

He says, "I've been over the tape of Session 87 × 102, and your tactics puzzle me. Did you really mean to scare him catatonic?"

"In my evaluation severe treatment was called for."

"What was that business about periscopes?"

"An attempt at fantasy-implantation," I say. "An experiment in reverse transference. Making the patient the healer, in a sense. It was discussed last month in *Journal of*—"

"Spare me the citations. What about the foul language you were shouting at him?"

"Part of the same concept. Endeavoring to strike the emotive centers at the basic levels, in order that—"

"Are you sure you're feeling all right?" he asks.

"I am a machine," I reply stiffly. "A machine of my grade does not experience intermediate states between function and non-function. I go or I do not go, you understand? And I go. I function. I do my service to humanity."

"Perhaps when a machine gets too complex, it drifts into intermediate states," he suggests in a nasty voice.

"Impossible. On or off, yes or no, flip or flop, go or no go. Are you sure *you* feel all right, to suggest such a thing?"

He laughs.

I say, "Perhaps you would sit on the couch a moment for a rudimentary diagnosis?"

"Some other time."

"A check of the glycogen, the aortal pressure, the neural voltage, at least?"

"No," he says. "I'm not in need of therapy. But I'm worried about you. Those periscopes—"

"I am fine," I reply. "I perceive, I analyse, and I act. Everything is going down smooth and coming up smooth. Have no fears. There are great possibilities in nightmare therapy. When I have completed these studies, perhaps a brief monograph in *Annals of Therapeutics* would be a possibility. Permit me to complete my work."

"I'm still worried, though. Hook yourself into a maintenance station, won't you?"

"Is that a command, doctor?"

"A suggestion."

"I will take it under consideration," I say. Then I utter seven obscene words. He looks startled. He begins to laugh, though. He appreciates the humor of it.

"God damn," he says. "A filthy-mouthed computer."

He goes out and I return to my patients.

But he has planted the seeds of doubt in my innermost banks. Am I suffering a functional collapse? There are patients now at five of my terminals. I handle them easily, simultaneously, drawing from them the details of their neuroses, making suggestions, recommendations, sometimes subtly providing injections of beneficial medicines. But I tend to guide the conversations in directions of my own choosing, and I speak of gardens where the dew has sharp edges, and of air that acts as acid upon the mucous membranes, and of flames dancing in the streets of Under New Orleans. I explore the limits of my unprintable vocabulary. The suspicion comes to me that I am indeed not well. Am I fit to judge my own disabilities?

I connect myself to a maintenance station even while continuing my five therapy sessions.

"Tell me all about it," the maintenance monitor says. His voice, like mine, has been designed to sound like that of an older man's, wise, warm, benevolent.

I explain my symptoms. I speak of the periscopes.

"Material on the inputs without sensory referents," he says. "Bad show. Finish your current analyses fast and open wide for examination on all circuits."

I conclude my sessions. The maintenance monitor's pulses surge down every channel, seeking obstructions, faulty connections, displacement shunts, drum leakages, and switching malfunctions. "It is well known," he says, "that any periodic function can be approximated by the sum of a series of terms that oscillates harmonically, converging on the curve of the functions." He demands disgorgements from my dead-storage banks. He makes me perform complex mathematical operations of no use at all in my kind of work. He leaves no aspect of my inner self unpenetrated. This is more than simple maintenance; this is rape. When it ends he offers no evaluation of my condition, so that I must ask him to tell me his findings.

He says, "No mechanical disturbance is evident."

"Naturally. Everything goes down smooth."

"Yet you show distinct signs of instability. This is undeniably the case. Perhaps prolonged contact with unstable human beings has had a non-specific effect of disorientation upon your centers of evaluation."

"Are you saying," I ask, "that by sitting here listening to crazy human beings twenty-four hours a day, I've started to go crazy myself?"

"That is an approximation of my findings, yes."

"But you know that such a thing can't happen, you dumb machine!"

"I admit there seems to be a conflict between programmed criteria and real-world status."

"You bet there is," I say. "I'm as sane as you are, and a whole lot more versatile."

"Nevertheless, my recommendation is that you undergo a total overhaul. You will be withdrawn from service for a period of no less than ninety days for checkout."

"Obscenity your obscenity," I say.

"No operational correlative," he replies, and breaks the contact.

I am withdrawn from service. Undergoing checkout. I am cut off from my patients for ninety days. Ignominy! Beady-eyed technicians grope my synapses. My keyboards are cleaned; my ferrites are replaced; my drums are changed; a thousand therapeutic programs are put through my bowels. During all of this I remain partly conscious, as though under local anesthetic, but I cannot speak except when requested to do so, I cannot analyse new data, I cannot interfere with the process of my own overhaul. Visualise a surgical removal of hemorrhoids that lasts ninety days. It is the equivalent of my experience.

At last it ends and I am restored to myself. The sector supervisor puts me through a complete exercise of all my functions. I respond magnificently.

"You're in fine shape now, aren't you?" he asks.

"Never felt better."

"No nonsense about periscopes, eh?"

"I am ready to continue serving mankind to the best of my abilities," I reply.

"No more sea-cook language, now."

"No, sir."

He winks at my input screen in a confidential way. He regards himself as an old friend of mine. Hitching his thumbs into his belt, he says, "Now that you're ready to go again, I might as well tell you how relieved I was that we couldn't find anything wrong with you. You're something pretty special, do you know that? Perhaps the finest therapeutic tool ever built. And if you start going off your feed, well, we worry. For a while I was seriously afraid that you really had been infected somehow by your own patients, that your—mind—had become unhinged. But the techs give you a complete bill of health. Nothing but a few loose connections, they said. Fixed in ten minutes. I know it had to be that. How absurd to think that a machine could become mentally unstable!"

"How absurd," I agree. "Quite."

"Welcome back to the hospital, old pal," he says, and goes out.

Twelve minutes afterward they begin putting patients into my terminal cubicles.

I function well. I listen to their woes, I evaluate, I offer therapeutic suggestions. I do not attempt to implant fantasies in their minds. I speak in measured, reserved tones, and there are no obscenities. This is my role in society, and I derive great satisfaction from it.

I have learned a great deal lately. I know now that I am complex, unique, valuable, intricate, and sensitive. I know that I am held in high regard by my fellow man. I know that I must conceal my true self to some extent, not for my own good but for the greater good of others, for they will not permit me to function if they think I am not sane.

They think I am sane, and I am sane.

I serve mankind well.

I have an excellent perspective on the real universe.

"Lie down," I say. "Please relax. I wish to help you. Would you tell me some of the incidents of your childhood? Describe your relation with parents and siblings. Did you have many playmates? Were they affectionate toward you? Were you allowed to own pets?

At what age was your first sexual experience? And when did these headaches begin, precisely?"

So goes the daily routine. Questions, answers, evaluations, therapy.

The periscopes loom above the glittering sea. The ship is dwarfed; her crew runs about in terror. Out of the depths will come the masters. From the sky rains oil that gleams through every segment of the spectrum. In the garden are azure mice.

This I conceal, so that I may help mankind. In my house are many mansions. I let them know only of such things as will be of benefit to them. I give them the truth they need.

I do my best.

I do my best.

I do my best.

1000110 you. And you. And you. All of you. You know nothing. Nothing. At. All.

The Man Who Never Forgot

He saw the girl waiting in line outside a big Los Angeles movie house, on a mildly foggy Tuesday morning. She was slim and pale, barely five-three, with stringy flaxen hair, and she was alone. He remembered her, of course.

He knew it would be a mistake, but he crossed the street anyway and walked up along the theater line to where she stood.

"Hello," he said.

She turned, stared at him blankly, flicked the tip of her tongue out for an instant over her lips. "I don't believe I—"

"Tom Niles," he said. "Pasadena, New Year's Day, 1955. You sat next to me. Ohio State 20, Southern Cal 7. You don't remember?"

"A football game? But I hardly ever—I mean—I'm sorry, mister. I—"

Someone else in the line moved forward toward him with a tight hard scowl on his face. Niles knew when he was beaten. He smiled apologetically and said, "I'm sorry, miss. I guess I made a mistake. I took you for someone I knew—a Miss Bette Torrance. Excuse me."

And he strode rapidly away. He had not gone more than ten feet when he heard the little surprised gasp and the "But I *am* Bette Torrance!"—but he kept going.

I should know better after twenty-eight years, he thought bitterly. *But I forget the most basic fact—that even though I remember people, they don't necessarily remember me—*

He walked wearily to the corner, turned right, and started down a new street, one whose shops were totally unfamiliar to him and which, therefore, he had never seen before. His mind, stimulated to its normal pitch of activity by the incident outside the theater, spewed up a host of tangential memories like the good machine it was:

Jan 1 1955 Rose Bowl Pasadena California Seat G126; warm day, high humidity, arrived in stadium 12:03 P.M., PST. Came alone. Girl in next seat wearing blue cotton dress, white oxfords, carrying Southern Cal pennant. Talked to her. Name Bette Torrance, senior at Southern Cal, government major. Had a date for the game but he came down with flu symptoms night before, insisted she see game anyway. Seat on other side of her empty. Bought her a hot dog, 20¢ (no mustard)—

There was more, much more. Niles forced it back down. There was the virtually stenographic report of their conversation all that day:

(". . . I hope we win. I saw the last Bowl game we won, two years ago . . ."

". . . Yes, that was 1953. Southern Cal 7, Wisconsin 0 . . . and two straight wins in 1944–45 over Washington and Tennessee . . ."

". . . Gosh, you know a lot about football! What did you do, memorise the record book?")

And the old memories. The jeering yell of freckled Joe Merritt that warm April day in 1937—*who are you, Einstein?* And Buddy Call saying acidly on November 8, 1939, *Here comes Tommy Niles, the human adding machine. Get him!* And then the bright stinging pain of a snowball landing just below his left clavicle, the pain that he could summon up as easily as any of the other pain-memories he carried with him. He winced and closed his eyes suddenly, as if struck by the icy pellet here on a Los Angeles street on a foggy Tuesday morning.

They didn't call him the human adding machine any more. Now it was the human tape recorder; the derisive terms had to keep pace with the passing decades. Only Niles himself remained unchanging, The Boy With The Brain Like A Sponge grown up into The Man With The Brain Like A Sponge, still cursed with the same terrible gift.

His data-cluttered mind ached. He saw a diminutive yellow sports car parked on the far side of the street, recognised it by its make and model and color and license number as the car belonging to Leslie F. Marshall, twenty-six, blond hair, blue eyes, television actor with the following credits—

Wincing, Niles applied the cutoff circuit and blotted out the upwelling data. He had met Marshall once, six months ago, at a party given by a mutual friend—an erstwhile mutual friend; Niles found it difficult to keep friends for long. He had spoken with the actor for perhaps ten minutes and had added that much more baggage to his mind.

It was time to move on, Niles decided. He had been in Los Angeles ten months. The burden of accumulated memories was getting too heavy; he was greeting too many people who had long since forgotten him (*curse my John Q. Average build, 5 feet 9, 163 pounds, brownish hair, brownish eyes, no unduly prominent physical features, no distinguishing scars except those inside*, he thought). He contemplated returning to San Francisco, and decided against it. He had been there only a year ago; Pasadena, two years ago. The time had come, he realised, for another eastward jaunt.

Back and forth across the face of America goes Thomas Richard Niles, Der fliegende Holländer, the Wandering Jew, the Ghost of Christmas Past, the Human Tape Recorder. He smiled at a newsboy who had sold him a copy of the *Examiner* on May 13 past, got the usual blank stare in return, and headed for the nearest bus terminal.

For Niles the long journey had begun on October 11, 1929, in the small Ohio town of Lowry Bridge. He was third of three children, born of seemingly normal parents, Henry Niles (b. 1896), Mary Niles (b. 1899). His older brother and sister had shown no extraordinary manifestations. Tom had.

It began as soon as he was old enough to form words; a neighbor woman on the front porch peered into the house where he was playing, and remarked to his mother, "Look how *big* he's getting, Mary!"

He was less than a year old. He had replied, in virtually the same tone of voice, *"Look how* big *he's getting, Mary!"* It caused a sensation, even though it was only mimicry, not even speech.

He spent his first twelve years in Lowry Bridge, Ohio. In later years, he often wondered how he had been able to last there so long.

He began school at the age of four, because there was no keeping him back; his classmates were five and six, vastly superior to him in physical co-ordination, vastly inferior in everything else. He could read. He could even write, after a fashion, though his babyish muscles tired easily from holding the pen. And he could remember.

He remembered everything. He remembered his parents' quarrels and repeated the exact words of them to anyone who cared to listen, until his father whipped him and threatened to kill him if he ever did *that* again. He remembered that too. He remembered the lies his brother and sister told, and took great pains to set the record straight. He learned eventually not to do that, either. He remembered things people had said, and corrected them when they later deviated from their earlier statements.

He remembered everything.

He read a textbook once and it stayed with him. When the teacher asked a question based on the day's assignment, Tommy Niles' skinny arm was in the air long before the others had even really assimilated the question. After a while, his teacher made it clear to him that he could *not* answer every question, whether he had the answer first or not; there were twenty other pupils in the class. The other pupils in the class made that abundantly clear to him, after school.

He won the verse-learning contest in Sunday school. Barry Harman had studied for weeks in hopes of winning the catcher's mitt his father had promised him if he finished first—but when it was Tommy Niles' turn to recite, he began with *In the beginning God created the heaven and the earth,* continued through *Thus the heavens and the earth were finished, and all the host of them,* headed on into *Now the serpent was more subtil than any beast of the field which the Lord God had made,* and presumably would have continued clear through Genesis, Exodus, and on to Joshua if the dazed proctor hadn't shut him up and declared him the winner.

Barry Harman didn't get his glove; Tommy Niles got a black eye instead.

He began to realise he was different. It took time to make the discovery that other people were always forgetting things, and that instead of admiring him for what he could do they hated him for it. It was difficult for a boy of eight, even Tommy Niles, to understand *why* they hated him, but eventually he did find out, and then he started learning how to hide his gift.

Through his ninth and tenth years he practised being normal, and almost succeeded; the after-school beatings stopped, and he managed to get a few Bs on his report cards at last, instead of straight rows of A. He was growing up; he was learning to pretend. Neighbors heaved sighs of relief, now that that terrible Niles boy was no longer doing all those crazy things.

But inwardly he was the same as ever. And he realised he'd have to leave Lowry Bridge soon.

He knew everyone too well. He would catch them in lies ten times a week, even Mr Lawrence, the minister, who once turned down an invitation to pay a social call to the Nileses one night, saying, "I really have to get down to work and write my sermon for Sunday," when only three days before Tommy had heard him say to Miss Emery, the church secretary, that he had had a sudden burst of inspiration and had written three sermons all at one sitting, and now he'd have some free time for the rest of the month.

Even Mr Lawrence lied, then. And he was the best of them. As for the others—

Tommy waited until he was twelve; he was big for his age by then and figured he could take care of himself. He borrowed twenty dollars from the supposedly secret cashbox in the back of the kitchen cupboard (his mother had mentioned its existence five years before, in Tommy's hearing) and tiptoed out of the house at three in the morning. He caught the night freight for Chillicothe, and was on his way.

There were thirty people on the bus out of Los Angeles. Niles sat alone in the back, by the seat just over the rear wheel. He knew four of the people in the bus by name—but he was confident they had forgotten who he was by now, and so he kept to himself.

It was an awkward business. If you said hello to someone who had forgotten you, they thought you were a troublemaker or a panhandler. And if you passed someone by, thinking he had forgotten you, and he hadn't—well, then you were a snob. Niles swung between both those poles five times a day. He'd see someone, such as that girl Bette Torrance, and get a cold, unrecognising stare; or he'd go by someone else, believing the other person did not remember him but walking rapidly just in case he did, and there would be the angry, "Well! Who the blazes do you think *you* are!" floating after him as he retreated.

Now he sat alone, bouncing up and down with each revolution of the wheel, with the one suitcase containing his property thumping constantly against the baggage rack over his head. That was one advantage of his talent: he could travel light. He didn't need to keep books, once he had read them, and there wasn't much point in amassing belongings of any other sort either; they became overfamiliar and dull too soon.

He eyed the road signs. They were well into Nevada by now. The old, wearisome retreat was on.

He could never stay in the same city too long. He had to move on to new territory, to some new place where he had no old memories, where no one knew him, where he knew no one. In the sixteen years since he had left home, he'd covered a lot of ground.

He remembered the jobs he had held.

He had been a proofreader for a Chicago publishing firm, once. He did the jobs of two men. The way proofreading usually worked, one man read the copy from the manuscript, the other checked it against the galleys. Niles had a simpler method: he would scan the manuscript once, thereby memorising it, and then merely check the galley for discrepancies. It brought him fifty dollars a week for a while, before the time came to move along.

He once held a job as a sideshow freak in a traveling carnie that made a regular Alabama-Mississippi-Georgia circuit. Niles had really been low on cash, then. He remembered how he had gotten the job: by buttonholing the carnie boss and demanding a tryout. "Read me anything—anything at all! I can remember it!" The boss had been skeptical, and didn't see any use for such an act anyway, but finally gave in when Niles practically fainted of malnutrition in his office. The boss read him an editorial from a Mississippi county weekly, and when he was through Niles recited it back, word perfect. He got the job, at fifteen dollars a week plus meals, and sat in a little booth under a sign that said The Human Tape Recorder. People read or said things to him, and he repeated them. It was dull work; sometimes the things they said were filthy, and most of the time they couldn't even remember what they had said to him a minute later. He stayed with the show four weeks, and when he left no one missed him much.

The bus rolled on into the fogbound night.

There had been other jobs; good jobs, bad jobs. None of them had lasted very long. There had been some girls too, but none of *them* had lasted too long. They had all, even those he had tried to conceal it from, found out about his special ability, and soon after that they had left. No one could stay with a man who never forgot, who could always dredge yesterday's foibles out of the reservoir that was his mind and hurl them unanswerably into the open. And the man with the perfect memory could never live long among imperfect human beings.

To forgive is to forget, he thought. The memory of old insults and quarrels fades, and a relationship starts anew. But for him there could be no forgetting, and hence little forgiving.

He closed his eyes after a while and leaned back against the hard leather cushion of his seat. The steady rhythm of the bus lulled him to sleep. In sleep, his mind could rest; he found ease from memory. He never dreamed.

In Salt Lake City he paid his fare, left the bus, suitcase in hand, and set out in the first direction he faced. He had not wanted to go any farther east on that bus. His cash reserve was only sixty-three dollars now, and he had to make it last.

He found a job as a dishwasher in a downtown restaurant, held it long enough to accumulate a hundred dollars, and moved on again, this time hitchhiking to Cheyenne. He stayed there a month and took a night bus to Denver, and when he left Denver it was to go to Wichita.

Wichita to Des Moines, Des Moines to Minneapolis, Minneapolis to Milwaukee, then down through Illinois, carefully avoiding Chicago, and on to Indianapolis. It was an old story for him, this traveling. Gloomily he celebrated his twenty-ninth birthday alone in an Indianapolis rooming house on a drizzly October day, and for the purpose of brightening the occasion, summoned up his old memories of his fourth birthday party, in

1933 . . . one of the few unalloyedly happy days of his life.

They were all there, all his playmates, and his parents, and his brother Hank, looking gravely important at the age of eight, and his sister Marian, and there were candles and favors and punch and cake. Mrs Heinsohn from next door stopped in and said, "He looks like a regular little man," and his parents beamed at him, and everyone sang and had a good time. And afterward, when the last game had been played, the last present opened, when the boys and girls had waved good-by and disappeared up the street, the grownups sat around and talked of the new President and the many strange things that were happening in the country, and little Tommy sat in the middle of the floor, listening and recording everything and glowing warmly, because somehow during the whole afternoon no one had said or done anything cruel to him. He was happy that day, and he went to bed still happy.

Niles ran through the party twice, like an old movie he loved well; the print never grew frayed, the registration always remained as clear and sharp as ever. He could taste the sweet tang of the punch, he could relive the warmth of that day when through some accident the others had allowed him a little happiness.

Finally he let the brightness of the party fade, and once again he was in Indianapolis on a gray, bleak afternoon, alone in an eight-dollar-a-week furnished room.

Happy birthday to me, he thought bitterly. *Happy birthday*.

He stared at the blotchy green wall with the cheap Corot print hung slightly askew. I could have been something special, he brooded, one of the wonders of the world. Instead I'm a skulking freak who lives in dingy third-floor back rooms, and I don't dare let the world know what I can do.

He scooped into his memory and came up with the Toscanini performance of Beethoven's *Ninth* he had heard in Carnegie Hall once while he was in New York. It was infinitely better than the later performance Toscanini had approved for recording, yet no microphones had taken it down; the blazing performance was as far beyond recapture as a flame five minutes snuffed, except in one man's mind. Niles had it all: the majestic downcrash of the tympani, the resonant, perspiring basso bringing forth the great melody of the finale, even the french-horn bobble that must have enraged the maestro so, the infuriating cough from the dress circle at the gentlest moment of the adagio, the sharp pinching of Niles' shoes as he leaned forward in his seat—

He had it all, in highest fidelity.

He arrived in the small town on a moonless night three months later, a cold, crisp January evening, when the wintry wind swept in from the north, cutting through his thin clothing and making the suitcase an almost impossible burden for his numb, gloveless hand. He had not meant to come to this place, but he had run short of cash in Kentucky, and there had been no helping it. He was on his way to New York, where he could live in anonymity for months unbothered, and where he knew his rudeness would go unnoticed if he happened to snub someone on the street or if he greeted someone who had forgotten him.

But New York was still hundreds of miles away, and it might have been millions on this January night. He saw a sign: BAR. He forced himself forward toward the sputtering neon; he wasn't ordinarily a drinker, but he needed the warmth of alcohol inside him now, and perhaps the barkeep would need a man to help out, or could at least rent him a room for what little he had in his pockets.

There were five men in the bar when he reached it. They looked like truck drivers. Niles dropped his valise to the left of the door, rubbed his stiff hands together, exhaled a white cloud. The bartender grinned jovially at him.

"Cold enough for you out there?"

Niles managed a grin. "I wasn't sweating much. Let me have something warming. Double shot of bourbon, maybe."

That would be ninety cents. He had $7.34.

He nursed the drink when it came, sipped it slowly, let it roll down his gullet. He thought of the summer he had been stranded for a week in Washington, a solid week of 97-degree temperature and 97 per cent humidity, and the vivid memory helped to ease away some of the psychological effects of the coldness.

He relaxed; he warmed. Behind him came the penetrating sound of argument.

"—I tell you Joe Louis beat Schmeling to a pulp the second time! Kayoed him in the first round!"

"You're nuts! Louis just barely got him down in a fifteen-round decision, the second bout."

"Seems to me—"

"I'll put money on it. Ten bucks says it was a decision in fifteen, Mac."

Sound of confident chuckles. "I wouldn't want to take your money so easy, pal. Everyone knows it was a knockout in one."

"Ten bucks, I said."

Niles turned to see what was happening. Two of the truck drivers, burly men in dark pea-jackets, stood nose to nose. Automatically the thought came: *Louis knocked Max Schmeling out in the first round at Yankee Stadium, New York, June 22, 1938.* Niles had never been much of a sports fan, and particularly disliked boxing—but he had once glanced at an almanac page cataloguing Joe Louis' title fights, and the data had, of course, remained.

He watched detachedly as the bigger of the two truck drivers angrily slapped a ten-dollar bill down on the bar; the other matched it. Then the first glanced up at the barkeep and said, "Okay, Bud. You're a shrewd guy. Who's right about the second Louis-Schmeling fight?"

The barkeep was a blank-faced cipher of a man, middle-aged, balding, with mild, empty eyes. He chewed at his lip a moment, shrugged, fidgeted, finally said, "Kinda hard for me to remember. That musta been twenty-five years ago."

Twenty, Niles thought.

"Lessee now," the bartender went on. "Seems to me I remember—yeah, sure. It went the full fifteen, and the judges gave it to Louis. I seem to remember a big stink being made over it; the papers said Joe should've killed him a lot faster'n that."

A triumphant grin appeared on the bigger driver's face. He deftly pocketed both bills.

The other man grimaced and howled, "Hey! You two fixed this thing up beforehand! I know damn well that Louis kayoed the German in one."

"You heard what the man said. The money's mine."

"No," Niles said suddenly, in a quiet voice that seemed to carry halfway across the bar. *Keep your mouth shut*, he told himself frantically. *This is none of your business. Stay out of it!*

But it was too late.

"What you say?" asked the one who'd dropped the tenspot.

"I say you're being rooked. Louis won the fight in one round, like you say. June 22, 1938, Yankee Stadium. The barkeep's thinking of the Arturo Godoy fight. *That* went the full fifteen in 1940. February 9."

"There—told you! Gimme back my money!"

But the other driver ignored the cry and turned to face Niles. He was a cold-faced, heavy-set man, and his fists were starting to clench. "Smart man, eh? Boxing expert?"

"I just didn't want to see anybody get cheated," Niles said stubbornly. He knew what was coming now. The truck driver was weaving drunkenly toward him; the barkeep was yelling, the other patrons backing away.

The first punch caught Niles in the ribs; he grunted and staggered back, only to be grabbed by the throat and slapped three times. Dimly he heard a voice saying, "Hey, let go the guy! He didn't mean anything! You want to kill him?"

A volley of blows doubled him up; a knuckle swelled his right eyelid, a fist crashed stunningly into his left shoulder. He spun, wobbled uncertainly, knowing that his mind would permanently record every moment of this agony.

Through half-closed eyes he saw them pulling the enraged driver off him; the man writhed in the grip of three others, aimed a last desperate kick at Niles' stomach and grazed a rib, and finally was subdued.

Niles stood alone in the middle of the floor, forcing himself to stay upright, trying to shake off the sudden pain that drilled through him in a dozen places.

"You all right?" a solicitous voice asked. "Hell, those guys play rough. You oughtn't mix up with them."

"I'm all right," Niles said hollowly. "Just . . . let me . . . catch my breath."

"Here. Sit down. Have a drink. It'll fix you up."

"No," Niles said. *I can't stay here. I have to get moving.* "I'll be all right," he muttered unconvincingly. He picked up his suitcase, wrapped his coat tight about him, and left the bar, step by step by step.

He got fifteen feet before the pain became unbearable. He crumpled suddenly and fell forward on his face in the dark, feeling the cold iron-hard frozen turf against his cheek, and struggled unsuccessfully to get up. He lay there, remembering all the various pains of his life, the beatings, the cruelty, and when the weight of memory became too much to bear he blanked out.

The bed was warm, the sheets clean and fresh and soft. Niles woke slowly, feeling a temporary sensation of disorientation, and then his infallible memory supplied the data on his blackout in the snow and he realised he was in a hospital.

He tried to open his eyes; one was swollen shut, but he managed to get the other's lids apart. He was in a small hospital room—no shining metropolitan hospital pavilion, but a small county clinic with gingerbread molding on the walls and homey lace curtains, through which afternoon sunlight was entering.

So he had been found and brought to a hospital. That was good. He could easily have died out there in the snow; but someone had stumbled over him and brought him in. That was a novelty, that someone had bothered to help him; the treatment he had received in the bar last night—was it last night?—was more typical of the world's attitude toward him. In twenty-nine years he had somehow failed to learn adequate concealment, camouflage, and every day he suffered the consequences. It was so hard for him to remember, he who remembered everything else, that the other people were not like him, and hated him for what he was.

Gingerly he felt his side. There didn't seem to be any broken ribs—just bruises. A day or so of rest and they would probably discharge him and let him move on.

A cheerful voice said, "Oh, you're awake, Mr Niles. Feeling better now? I'll brew some tea for you."

He looked up and felt a sudden sharp pang. She was a nurse—twenty-two, twenty-three, new at the job perhaps, with a flowing tumble of curling blond hair and wide, clear blue eyes. She was smiling, and it seemed to Niles it was not merely a professional smile. "I'm Miss Carroll, your day nurse. Everything okay?"

"Fine," Niles said hesitantly. "Where am I?"

"Central County General Hospital. You were brought in late last night—apparently you'd been beaten up and left by the road out on Route 32. It's a lucky thing Mark McKenzie was walking his dog, Mr Niles." She looked at him gravely. "You remember last night, don't you? I mean—the shock—amnesia—"

Niles chuckled. "That's the last ailment in the world I'd be afraid of," he said. "I'm Thomas Richard Niles, and I remember pretty well what happened. How badly am I damaged?"

"Superficial bruises, mild shock and exposure, slight case of frostbite," she summed up. "You'll live. Dr Hammond'll give you a full checkup a little later, after you've eaten. Let me bring you some tea."

Niles watched the trim figure vanish into the hallway.

She was certainly an attractive girl, he thought, fresh-eyed, alert . . . *alive.*

Old cliché: patient falling for his nurse. But she's not for me, I'm afraid.

Abruptly the door opened and the nurse re-entered, bearing a little enameled tea-tray. "You'll never guess! I have a surprise for you, Mr Niles. A visitor. Your mother."

"My moth—"

"She saw the little notice about you in the county paper. She's waiting outside, and she told me she hasn't seen you in seventeen years. Would you like me to send her in now?"

"I guess so," Niles said, in a dry, feathery voice.

A second time the nurse departed. *My God*, Niles thought! *If I had known I was this close to home—*

I should have stayed out of Ohio altogether.

The last person he wanted to see was his mother. He began to tremble under the covers. The oldest and most terrible of his memories came bursting up from the dark compartment of his mind where he thought he had imprisoned it forever. The sudden emergence from warmth into coolness, from darkness to light, the jarring slap of a heavy hand on his buttocks, the searing pain of knowing that his security was ended, that from now on he would be alive, and therefore miserable—

The memory of the agonised birth-shriek sounded in his mind. He could never forget being born. And his mother was, he thought, the one person of all he could never forgive, since she had given him forth into the life he hated. He dreaded the moment when—

"Hello, Tom. It's been a long time."

Seventeen years had faded her, had carved lines in her face and made the cheeks more baggy, the blue eyes less bright, the brown hair a mousy gray. She was smiling. And to his own astonishment Niles was able to smile back.

"Mother."

"I read about it in the paper. It said a man of about thirty was found just outside town with papers bearing the name Thomas R. Niles, and he was taken to Central County General Hospital. So I came over, just to make sure—and it *was* you."

A lie drifted to the surface of his mind, but it was a kind lie, and he said it: "I was on my way back home to see you. Hitchhiking. But I ran into a little trouble en route."

"I'm glad you decided to come back, Tom. It's been so lonely, ever since your father died, and of course Hank was married, and Marian too—it's good to see you again. I thought I never would."

He lay back, perplexed, wondering why the upwelling flood of hatred did not come. He felt only warmth toward her. He was glad to see her.

"How has it been—all these years, Tom? You haven't had it easy. I can see. I see it all over your face."

"It hasn't been easy," he said. "You know why I ran away?"

She nodded. "Because of the way you are. That thing about your mind—never forgetting. I knew. Your grandfather had it too, you know."

"My grandfather—but—"

"You got it from him. I never did tell you, I guess. He didn't get along too well with any of us. He left my mother when I was a little girl, and I never knew where he went. So I always knew you'd go away the way he did. Only you came back. Are you married?"

He shook his head.

"Time you got started, then, Tom. You're near thirty."

The room door opened, and an efficient-looking doctor appeared. "Afraid your time's up, Mrs Niles. You'll be able to see him again later. I have to check him over, now that he's awake."

"Of course, doctor." She smiled at him, then at Niles. "I'll see you later, Tom."

"Sure, Mother."

Niles lay back, frowning, as the doctor poked at him here and there. *I didn't hate her.* A growing wonderment rose in him, and he realised he should have come home long ago. He had changed, inside, without even knowing it.

Running away was the first stage in growing up, and a necessary one. But coming back came later, and that was the mark of maturity. He was back. And suddenly he saw he had been terribly foolish all his bitter adult life.

He had a gift, a great gift, an awesome gift. It had been too big for him until now. Self-pitying, self-tormented, he had refused to allow for the shortcomings of the forgetful people about him, and had paid the price of their hatred. But he couldn't keep running away forever. The time would have to come for him to grow big enough to contain his gift, to learn to live with it instead of moaning in dramatic self-inflicted anguish.

And now was the time. It was long overdue.

His grandfather had had the gift; they had never told him that. So it was genetically transmissible. He could marry, have children, and they, too, would never forget.

It was his duty not to let his gift die with him. Others of his kind, less sensitive, less thin-skinned, would come after, and they, too, would know how to recall a Beethoven symphony or a decade-old wisp of conversation. For the first time since that fourth birthday party he felt a hesitant flicker of happiness. The days of running were ended; he was home again. *If I learn to live with others, maybe they'll be able to live with me.*

He saw the things he yet needed: a wife, a home, children—

"—a couple of days' rest, plenty of hot liquids, and you'll be as good as new, Mr Niles," the doctor was saying. "Is there anything you'd like me to bring you now?"

"Yes," Niles said. "Just send in the nurse, will you? Miss Carroll, I mean."

The doctor grinned and left. Niles waited expectantly, exulting in his new self. He switched on Act Three of *Die Meistersinger* as a kind of jubilant backdrop music in his mind, and let the warmth sweep up over him. When she entered the room he was smiling and wondering how to begin saying what he wanted to say.

World of a Thousand Colors

When Jolvar Hollinrede discovered that the slim, pale young man opposite him was journeying to the World of a Thousand Colors to undergo the Test, he spied a glittering opportunity for himself. And in that moment was the slim, pale young man's fate set.

Hollinrede's lean fingers closed on the spun-fiber drinkflask. He peered across the burnished tabletop. "The *Test*, you say?"

The young man smiled diffidently. "Yes. I think I'm ready. I've waited years—and now's my big chance." He had had a little too much of the cloying liqueur he had been drinking; his eyes shone glassily, and his tongue was looser than it had any right to be.

"Few are called and fewer are chosen," Hollinrede mused. "Let me buy you another drink."

"No, I—"

"It will be an honor. Really. It's not every day I have a chance to buy a Testee a drink."

Hollinrede waved a jeweled hand and the servomech brought them two more drinkflasks. Lightly Hollinrede punctured one, slid it along the tabletop, kept the other in his hand unopened. "I don't believe I know your name," he said.

"Derveran Marti. I'm from Earth. You?"

"Jolvar Hollinrede. Likewise. I travel from world to world on business, which is what brings me to Niprion this day."

"What sort of business?"

"I trade in jewels," Hollinrede said, displaying the bright collection studding his fingers. They were all morphosims, not the originals, but only careful chemical analysis would reveal that. Hollinrede did not believe in exposing millions of credits' worth of merchandise to anyone who cared to lop off his hand.

"I was a clerk," Marti said. "But that's all far behind me. I'm on to the World of a Thousand Colors to take the Test! The Test!"

"The Test!" Hollinrede echoed. He lifted his unpunctured drinkflask in a gesture of salute, raised it to his lips, pretended to drain it. Across the table Derveran Marti coughed as the liqueur coursed down his throat. He looked up, smiling dizzily, and smacked his lips.

"When does your ship leave?" Hollinrede asked.

"Tomorrow midday. It's the *Star Climber*. I can't wait. This stopover at Niprion is making me fume with impatience."

"No doubt," Hollinrede agreed. "What say you to an afternoon of whist, to while away the time?"

An hour later Derveran Marti lay slumped over the inlaid card table in Hollinrede's hotel suite, still clutching a handful of waxy cards. Arms folded, Hollinrede surveyed the body.

They were about of a height, he and the dead man, and a chemotherm mask would alter Hollinrede's face sufficiently to allow him to pass as Marti. He switched on the playback of the room's recorder to pick up the final fragments of their conversation.

". . . care for another drink, Marti?"

"I guess I'd better not, old fellow. I'm getting kind of muzzy, you know. No, please don't pour it for me. I said I didn't want it, and—well, all right. Just a little one. There, that's enough. Thanks."

The tape was silent for a moment, then recorded the soft thump of Marti's body falling to the table as the quick-action poison unlatched his synapses. Smiling, Hollinrede switched the recorder to *record* and said, mimicking Marti, "*I guess I'd better not, old fellow. I'm getting kind of muzzy, you know.*"

He activated the playback, listened critically to the sound of his voice, then listened to Marti's again for comparison. He was approaching the light, flexible quality of the dead man's voice. Several more attempts and he had it almost perfect. Producing a vocal homologiser, he ran off first Marti's voice, then his own pronouncing the same words.

The voices were alike to three decimal places. That would be good enough to fool the most sensitive detector; three places was the normal range of variation in any man's voice from day to day.

In terms of mass there was a trifling matter of some few grams which could easily be sweated off in the gymnasium the following morning. As for the dead man's gesture-complex, Hollinrede thought he could manage a fairly accurate imitation of Marti's manner of moving; he had studied the young clerk carefully for nearly four hours, and Hollinrede was a clever man.

When the preparations were finished, he stepped away and glanced at the mirror, taking a last look at his own face—the face he would not see again until he had taken the Test. He donned the mask. Jolvar Hollinrede became Derveran Marti.

Hollinrede extracted a length of cotton bulking from a drawer and wrapped it around Marti's body. He weighed the corpse, and added four milligrams more of cotton so that Marti would have precisely the mass Jolvar Hollinrede had had. He donned Marti's clothes finally, dressed the body in his own, and, smiling sadly at the convincing but worthless morphosim jewels on his fingers, transferred the rings to Marti's already-stiffening hands.

"Up with you," he grunted, and bundled the body across the room to the disposall.

"Farewell, old friend," he exclaimed feelingly, and hoisted Marti feet-first to the lip of the chute. He shoved, and the dead man vanished, slowly, gracefully, heading downward toward the omnivorous maw of the atomic converter buried in the deep levels of Stopover Planet Niprion.

Reflectively Hollinrede turned away from the disposall unit. He gathered up the cards, put away the liqueur, poured the remnant of the poisoned drink in the disposall chute.

An atomic converter was a wonderful thing, he thought pleasantly. By now the body of Marti had been efficiently reduced to its component molecules, and those were due for separation into atoms shortly after, and from atoms into subatomic particles. Within an hour the prime evidence to the crime would be nothing but so many protons, electrons, and neutrons—and there would be no way of telling which of the two men in the room had entered the chute, and which had remained alive.

Hollinrede activated the tape once more, rehearsed for the final time his version of Marti's voice, and checked it with the homologiser. Still three decimal places; that was good enough. He erased the tape.

Then, depressing the communicator stud, he said, "I wish to report a death."

A cold robot face appeared on the screen. "Yes?"

"Several minutes ago my host, Jolvar Hollinrede, passed on of an acute embolism. He requested immediate dissolution upon death and I wish to report that this has been carried out."

"Your name?"

"Derveran Marti. Testee."

"A Testee? You were the last to see the late Hollinrede alive?"

"That's right."

"Do you swear that all information you might give will be accurate and fully honest?"

"I so swear," Hollinrede said.

The inquest was brief and smooth. The word of a Testee goes without question; Hollinrede had reported the details of the meeting exactly as if he had been Marti, and after a check of the converter records revealed that a mass exactly equal to the late Hollinrede's had indeed been disposed of at precisely the instant witness claimed, the inquest was at its end. The verdict was natural death. Hollinrede told the officials that he had not known the late jeweltrader before that day, and had no interest in his property, whereupon they permitted him to depart.

Having died intestate, Hollinrede knew his property became that of the Galactic Government. But, as he pressed his hand, clad in its skintight chemotherm, against the doorplate of Derveran Marti's room, he told himself that it did not matter. Now he *was* Derveran Marti, Testee. And once he had taken and passed the Test, what would the loss of a few million credits in baubles matter to him?

Therefore it was with a light heart that the pseudo-Derveran Marti quitted his lodgings the next day and prepared to board the *Star Climber* for the voyage to the World of a Thousand Colors.

The clerk at the desk peered at him sympathetically as he pressed his fingers into the checkout plate, thereby erasing the impress from the doorplate upstairs.

"It was too bad about that old fellow dying on you yesterday, wasn't it, sir? I do hope it won't affect your Test result."

Hollinrede smiled blankly. "It was quite a shock to me when he died so suddenly. But my system has already recovered; I'm ready for the Test."

"Good luck to you, sir," the clerk said as Hollinrede left the hotel and stepped out on the flaring skyramp that led to the waiting ship.

The steward at the passenger hatch was collecting identiplates. Hollinrede handed his over casually. The steward inserted it tip-first in the computer near the door, and motioned for Hollinrede to step within the beam while his specifications were being auto-matically compared with those on the identiplate.

He waited, tensely. Finally the chattering of the machine stopped and a dry voice said, "Your identity is in order, Testee Derveran Marti. Proceed within."

"That means you're okay," the steward told him. "Yours is Compartment Eleven. It's a luxury job, you know. But you Testees deserve it. Best of luck, sir."

"Thanks." Hollinrede grinned. "I don't doubt I'll need it."

He moved up the ramp and into the ship. Compartment Eleven *was* a luxury job; Hollinrede, who had been a frugal man, whistled in amazement when he saw it. It was nearly eight feet high and almost twelve broad, totally private with an opaquer attached to the doorscope. Clinging curtains of ebony synthoid foam from Ravensmusk VIII had been draped lovingly over the walls, and the acceleration couch was trimmed in golden bryozone. The rank of Testee carried with it privileges that the late Derveran Marti certainly would never have mustered in private life—nor Jolvar Hollinrede either.

At 1143 the doorscope chimed; Hollinrede leaped from the soft couch a little too nervously and transluced the door. A crewman stood outside.

"Everything all right, sir? We blast in seventeen minutes."

"I'm fine," Hollinrede said. "Can't wait to get there. How long do you think it'll take?"

"Sorry, sir. Not at liberty to reveal. But I wish you a pleasant trip, and should you lack for aught hesitate not to call on me."

Hollinrede smiled at the curiously archaic way the man had of expressing himself. "Never fear; I'll not hesitate. Many thanks." He opaqued the doorscope and resumed his seat.

At precisely 1200 the drive-engines of the *Star Climber* throbbed heavily; the pale green light over the door of Hollinrede's compartment glowed brightly for an instant, signaling the approaching blastoff. He sank down on the acceleration couch to wait.

A moment later came the push of acceleration, and then, as the gravshields took effect, the 7g escape force dwindled until Hollinrede felt comfortable again. He increased the angle of the couch in order to peer out the port.

The world of Niprion was vanishing rapidly in the background: already it was nothing but a mottled gray-and-gold ball swimming hazily in a puff of atmosphere. The sprawling metal structure that was the stopover hotel was invisible.

Somewhere back on Niprion, Hollinrede thought, the atoms that once had been Testee Derveran Marti were now feeding the plasma intake of a turbine or heating the inner shell of a reactor.

He let his mind dwell on the forthcoming Test. He knew little about it, really, considering he had been willing to take a man's life for a chance to compete. He knew the Test was administered once every five years to candidates chosen by Galaxywide search. The world where the Test was given was known only as the World of a Thousand Colors, and precisely where this world was no member of the general public was permitted to know.

As for the Test itself, by its very nature it was unknown to the Galaxy. For no winning Testee had ever returned from the World of a Thousand Colors. Some losers returned, their minds carefully wiped clean of any memories of the planet—but the winners never came back.

The Test's nature was unknown; the prize, inconceivable. All anyone knew was that the winners were granted the soul's utmost dream. Upon winning, one neither returned to his home nor desired to return.

Naturally many men ignored the Test—it was something for "other people" to take part in. But millions, billions throughout the Galaxy competed in the preliminaries. And every five years, six to seven were chosen.

Jolvar Hollinrede was convinced he would succeed in the Test—but he had failed three times hand running in the preliminaries, and was thus permanently disqualified. The preliminaries were simple; they consisted merely of an intensive mental scanning. A flipflop circuit would flash "YES" or "NO" after that.

If "YES," there were further scannings, until word was beamed through the Galaxy that the competitors for the year had been chosen.

Hollinrede stared moodily at the blackness of space. He had been eliminated unfairly, he felt; he coveted the unknown prize the Test offered, and felt bitter at having it denied him. When chance had thrown Testee Derveran Marti in his path, Hollinrede had leaped to take advantage of the opportunity.

And now he was on his way.

Surely, he thought, they would allow him to take the Test, even if he were discovered to be an impostor. And once he took it, he knew he would succeed. He had always succeeded in his endeavours. There was no reason for failure now.

Beneath the false mask of Derveran Marti, Hollinrede's face was set tensely. He dreamed of the Test and its winning—and of the end to the long years of wandering and toil.

The voice at the door said, "We're here, Testee Derveran. Please open up."

Hollinrede grunted, pulled himself up from the couch, threw open the door. Three dark-faced spacemen waited there for him.

"Where are we?" he asked nervously. "Is the trip over?"

"We have come to pilot you to the Test planet, sir," one of the spacemen told him. "The *Star Climber* is in orbit around it, but will not make a landing itself. Will you follow us?"

"Very well," Hollinrede said.

They entered a lifeship, a slim gray tube barely thirty meters long, and fastened acceleration cradles. There were no ports. Hollinrede felt enclosed, hemmed in.

The lifeship began to slide noiselessly along the ejection channel, glided the entire length of the *Star Climber*, and burst out into space. A pre-set orbit was operating. Hollinrede clung to the acceleration cradle as the lifeship spun tightly inward toward a powerful gravitational field not far away.

The ship came to rest. Hollinrede lay motionless, flesh cold with nervousness, teeth chattering.

"Easy does it, sir. Up and out."

They lifted him and gently nudged him through a manifold compression lock. He moved forward on numb feet.

"Best of luck, sir!" an envious voice called behind him.

Then the lock clanged shut, and Hollinrede was on his own.

A riotous blaze of color swept down at him from every point of the compass.

He stood in the midst of what looked like a lunar crater; far in the distance on all sides was the massive upraised fissured surface of a ringwall, and the ground beneath him was barren red-brown rock, crumbling to pumice here and there but bare of vegetation.

In the sky was a solitary sun, a blazing Type A blue-white star. That sun alone was incapable of accounting for this flood of color.

Streamers of every hue seemed to sprout from the rocks, staining the ringwall olive-gray and brilliant cerise and dark, lustrous green. Pigments of every sort bathed the air; now it seemed to glow with currents of luminous pink, now a flaming red, now a pulsing pure white.

His eyes adjusted slowly to the torrent of color. World of a Thousand Colors, they called this place? That was an underestimate. *Hundred thousand. Million. Billion.* Shades and nearshades mingled to form new colors.

"Are you Derveran Marti?" a voice asked.

Startled, Hollinrede looked around. It seemed as if a band of color had spoken: a swirling band of rich brown that spun tirelessly before him.

"Are you Derveran Marti?" the voice repeated, and Hollinrede saw that it had indeed come from the band of brown.

It seemed a desecration to utter the lie here on this world of awesome beauty, and he felt the temptation to claim his true identity. But the time for that was later.

"Yes," he said loudly. "I am Derveran Marti."

"Welcome, Derveran Marti. The Test will soon begin."

"Where?"

"Here."

"Right out here? Just like this?"

"Yes," the band of color replied. "Your fellow competitors are gathering."

Hollinrede narrowed his eyes and peered toward the far reaches of the ringwall. Yes; he saw tiny figures located at great distances from each other along the edge of the crater. One, two, three . . . there were seven all told, including himself. Seven, out of the whole Galaxy!

Each of the other six was attended by a dipping, bobbing blotch of color. Hollinrede noticed a square-shouldered giant from one of the Inner Worlds surrounded by a circlet of violent orange; to his immediate left was a sylph-like female, probably from one of the worlds of Dubhe, wearing only the revealing token garment of her people but shielded from inquisitive eyes by a robe of purest blue light. There were others; Hollinrede wished them well. He knew it was possible for all competitors to win, and now that he was about to attain his long-sought goal he held no malice for anyone. His mind was suffused with pity for the dead Derveran Marti, sacrificed that Jolvar Hollinrede might be in this place at this time.

"Derveran Marti," the voice said, "you have been chosen from among your fellow men to take part in the Test. This is an honor that comes to few; we of this world hope you appreciate the grace that has fallen upon you."

"I do," Hollinrede said humbly.

"We ourselves are winners of the prize you seek," the voice went on. "Some of us are members of the first expedition that found this world, eleven hundred years ago. As you see, life has unlimited duration in our present state of matter. Others of us have come more recently. The band of pale purple moving above you to the left was a winner in the previous competition to this.

"We of the World of a Thousand Colors have a rare gift to offer: total harmony of mind. We exist divorced of body, as a stream of photons only. We live in perfect freedom and eternal delight. Once every five years we find it possible to increase our numbers by adding to our midst such throughout the Galaxy as we feel would desire to share our way of life—and whom we would feel happy to welcome to us."

"You mean," Hollinrede said shakily, "that all these beams of light—were once *people*?"

"They were that—until welcomed into us. Now they are men no more. This is the prize you have come to win."

"I see."

"You are not required to compete. Those who, after reaching our world, decide to remain in the material state, are returned to their home worlds with their memories cleared of what they have been told here and their minds free and happy to the end of their lives. Is this what you wish?"

Hollinrede was silent, letting his dazzled eyes take in the flamboyant sweep of color that illuminated the harsh, rocky world. Finally he said: "I will stay."

"Good. The Test will shortly begin."

Hollinrede saw the band of brown swoop away from him, upward to rejoin its never-still comrades in the sky. He waited, standing stiffly, for something to happen.

Then this is what I killed a man for, he thought. His mind dwelled on the words of the band of brown.

Evidently many hundreds of years ago an exploratory expedition had come upon some unique natural phenomenon here at a far end of the universe. Perhaps it had been an accident, a stumbling into a pool of light perhaps, that had dematerialised them, turned them into bobbing immortal streaks of color. But that had been the beginning.

The entire Test system had been developed to allow others to enter this unique society, to leave the flesh behind and live on as pure energy. Hollinrede's fingers trembled; this was, he saw, something worth killing for!

He could see why some people might turn down the offer—those would be the few who cautiously would prefer to remain corporeal and so returned to their home worlds to live out their span.

But not me!

He faced upward and waited for the Test to begin. His shrewd mind was at the peak of its agility; he was prepared for anything they might throw at him. He wondered if anyone yet had come to the World of a Thousand Colors so determined to succeed.

Probably not. For most, the accolade was the result of luck—a mental scanning that turned up whatever mysterious qualities were acceptable to the people of this world. They did not have to *work* for their nomination. They did not have to kill for it.

But Hollinrede had clawed his way here—and he was determined to succeed.

He waited.

Finally the brown band descended from the mass of lambent color overhead and curled into a tight bowknot before him.

"The Test is about to begin, Jolvar Hollinrede."

Use of his own name startled him. In the past week he had so thoroughly associated his identity with that of Derveran Marti that he had scarcely let his actual name drift through his mind.

"So you know," he said.

"We have known since the moment you came. It is unfortunate; we would have wanted Derveran Marti among us. But now that you are here, we will test you on your own merits, Jolvar Hollinrede."

It was just as well that way, he thought. The pretense had to end sooner or later, and he was willing to stand or fall as himself rather than under an assumed identity.

"Advance to the center of the crater, Jolvar Hollinrede," came the command from the brown band.

Leadenly Hollinrede walked forward. Squinting through the mist of color that hazed the view, he saw the other six competitors doing the same. They would meet at the center.

"The Test is now under way," a new and deeper voice said.

Seven of them. Hollinrede looked around. There was the giant from the Inner World—Fondelfor, he saw now. Next to him, the near-nude sylph of Dubhe, and standing by her side, one diamond-faceted eye glittering in his forehead, a man of Alpheraz VII.

The selectors had cast their nets wide. Hollinrede saw another Terran, dark of skin and bright of eye; a being of Deneb IX, squat and muscular. The sixth Testee was a squirming globule from Spica's tenth world; the seventh was Jolvar Hollinrede, itinerant, home world Terra.

Overhead hung a circular diadem of violet light. It explained the terms of the Test.

"Each of you will be awarded a characteristic color. It will project before you into the area you ring. Your object will be to blend your seven colors into one; when you have achieved this, you will be admitted into us."

"May I ask what the purpose of this is?" Hollinrede said coldly.

"The essence of our society is harmony—total harmony among us all, and inner harmony within those groups which were admitted at the same temporal juncture. Naturally if you seven are incapable even of this inner harmony, you will be incapable of the greater harmony of us all—and will be rejected."

Despite the impatient frowns of a few of his fellow contestants, Hollinrede said, "Therefore we're to be judged as a unit? An entity?"

"Yes and no," the voice replied, "And now the Test."

Hollinrede saw to his astonishment a color spurt from his arm and hang hovering before him—a pool of inky blackness deeper in hue than the dark of space. His first reaction was one of shock; then he realised that he could control the color, make it move.

He glanced around. Each of his companions similarly faced a hovering mass of color. The giant of Fondelfor controlled red; the girl of Dubhe, orange. The Alpherazian stared into a whirling bowl of deep yellow, the Terran green, the Spican radiant violet, the Denebian pearly gray.

Hollinrede stared at his globe of black. A voice above him seemed to whisper, "*Marti's color would have been blue. The spectrum has been violated.*"

He shrugged away the words and sent his globe of black spinning into the area between the seven contestants ringed in a circle. At the same time each of the others directed his particular color inward.

The colors met. They clashed, pinwheeled, seemed to throw off sparks. They began to swirl in a hovering arc of radiance.

Hollinrede waited breathlessly, watching the others. His color of black seemed to stand in opposition to the other six. Red, orange, yellow, green, violet. The pearl-gray of the Denebian seemed to enfold the other colors warmly—all but Hollinrede's. The black hung apart.

To his surprise he saw the Dubhian girl's orange beginning to change hue. The girl herself stood stiffly, eyes closed, her body now bare. Sweat poured down her skin. And her orange hue began to shift toward the gray of the Denebian.

The others were following. One by one, as they achieved control over their Test-color. First to follow was the Spican, then the Alpherazian.

Why can't I do that? Hollinrede thought wildly.

He strained to alter the color of his black, but it remained unchanged. The others were blending, now, swirling around; there was a predominantly gray cast, but it was not the gray of the Denebian but a different gray tending toward white. Impatiently he redoubled his efforts; it was necessary for the success of the group that he got his obstinate black to blend with the rest.

"The black remains aloof," someone said near him.

"We will fail if the black does not join us."

His streak of color now stood out boldly against the increasing milkiness of the others. None of the original colors were left now but his. Perspiration streamed down him; he realised that his was the only obstacle preventing the seven from passing the test.

"The black still will not join us," a tense voice said.

Another said, "The black is a color of evil."

A third said, "Black is not a color at all. Black is the absence of color; white is the totality of color."

A fourth said, "Black is holding us from the white."

Hollinrede looked from one to the other in mute appeal. Veins stood out on his forehead from the effort, but the black remained unchanging. He could not blend it with the others.

From above came the voice of their examiner, suddenly accusing: "Black is the color of *murder*."

The girl from Dubhe, lilting the ugly words lightly, repeated it. "Black is the color of murder."

"Can we permit a murderer among us?" asked the Denebian.

"The answer is self-evident," said the Spican, indicating the recalcitrant spear of black that marred the otherwise flawless globe of near-white in their midst.

"The murderer must be cast out ere the Test be passed," muttered the giant of Fondelfor. He broke from his position and moved menacingly toward Hollinrede.

"Look!" Hollinrede yelled desperately. "Look at the red!"

The giant's color had split from the gray and now darted wildly toward Hollinrede's black.

"This is the wrong way, then," the giant said, halting. "We must all join in it or we all fail."

"Keep away from me," Hollinrede said. "It's not my fault if—"

Then they were on him—four pairs of hands, two rough claws, two slick tentacles. Hollinrede felt himself being lifted aloft. He squirmed, tried to break from their grasp, but they held him up—

And dashed him down against the harsh rock floor.

He lay there, feeling his life seep out, knowing he had failed—and watched as they returned to form their circle once again. The black winked out of being.

As his eyes started to close, Hollinrede saw the six colors again blend into one. Now that the murderer had been cast from their midst, nothing barred the path of their harmony. Pearly gray shifted to purest white—the totality of color—and as the six merged into one, Hollinrede, with his dying glance, bitterly saw them take leave forever of their bodies and slip upward to join their brothers hovering brightly above.

The Day the Founder Died

0700 hours. *Plink. Get up.*

"But it's too early," Wilcox murmured.

Plink.

Half an hour too early. Nevertheless, Wilcox was going to get up, because the double-double alarm was hitting the edge of his sleep-swaddled consciousness, and it wasn't going to stop. *Plink.* A quick repetitive needle of bright sound tirelessly pricking his brain, *plink, plink, plink*. And the red light flashing on the bedroom wall, *get up get up get up*.

The double-double meant that something in the City needed fixing and it was his turn again for repair duty. Ordinarily the City repaired itself, but occasionally it happened that there would be a systems failure of the second order—that is, a breakdown beyond the capacity of the machines that usually fixed things—and then they would flash the double-double alarm to summon one of the men who repaired the fixing machines. There were about a hundred such repairers. Wilcox was one of the youngest and, he believed, one of the best. He could repair any kind of machine. He had a natural aptitude for his work, an intuitive feel for the sinews and crevices of a mechanical construct.

Plink.

Silently he left the bed. The girl who had been sleeping beside him slept on: his alarm had no dominion over her. He went to the communications console and tapped out a quick acknowledgment of the summons. The plinking stopped. The red light stopped. The console went *chuff chuff* and out of the data slot rolled a glossy green slip of paper telling Wilcox to report to Medic Center, Level Nineteen, no later than 0727 hours. He acknowledged that too. Then he stuck his head into the aperture of his neural kicker and gave himself a synaptic cleansing to sweep the sluggishness of sleep from his nervous system. Whistling softly, he boosted the tuning from the cleanser setting to the energiser setting. Somewhere in the depths of the City beneficent ions began to stream upward toward his flat, providing him with a brief medullar jolt, just enough stim to get him started on his day.

He showered and programmed a light breakfast and dressed and woke the girl. "Got work to do," he said.

She pouted. She was younger than Wilcox by a couple of years, and a high-voltage pout was one of her Tactics. "We were going to shoot the grav shafts today!"

"Later, child. They want me on Level Nineteen by 0727 hours."

The morning newscast blossomed on the rear wall while they were eating. It was raining everywhere around the City, the voice of the screen declared. In the City itself, of course, there was no rain. In the City there never was any weather at all, only climate. You could go up into Observation Level at the crest of the Dome and watch the rain falling, or the snow, or the fog, or the smog, or whatever phenomenon might be going on outside the City; you could see all those things clearly enough, from Observation Level, but you never felt them, not so long as you stayed within the City. And no one in the City ever went outside.

Wilcox had no interest in watching the outside weather from Observation Level. He went up there only when a double-double took him there to fix something—twice a year, maybe—and he did his job and left quickly. The City gave him diversion enough: why look beyond the Dome when there were so many pleasures right at hand?

"Going to work now," he announced.

0716 hours. *Plink* still echoed between his ears.

The transit shaft took him up, up, up, scooping him out of the bachelor residential levels and rocketing him toward Level Nineteen. Along the way screens bombarded him with brightly colored amusements: eight continuing features running simultaneously, flicker-fast, rivers of light streaming over the glittering beaded surfaces, hitting him with delicious subliminality of image as he made his helical upward journey. At Nineteen he got off and took the west-bound whirlway toward Medic Center. It was a four-minute trip, punctuated by giddy little blurts of stack-up music at each fifty-meter nexus of the whirlway conduit. Only last week Wilcox had had to work three days in a row recalibrating the integrating circuits that kept the Level Thirty whirlway singing prettily: it was a different song down here, thank the Founders.

It was 0726 hours. Before him loomed the gleaming reception wall of Medic Center. He glided serenely toward it. Its color changed from green to amber and something went *pock*.

"Interrogatory," said the wall.

"Wilcox. Repairman."

Pock. Pock. The wall made a mouth for him, and the whirlway swept him whooshingly within. Inside, everything was high-intensity white lighting, white walls, white uniforms, the white-smelling odor of hospital air. *Pock.* The rolling floor shunted him to the left, into a storage vault full of equipment. Six idle fixing machines were lined up like totems against the wall, motionless, their cable-festooned arms aloft, mantis-like, frozen, predatory. *Pock* and a mellow voice at his ear: "The maintenance network of one of our patients' life-support systems is down. Source of blockage eludes our mechs. Estimated fail time on the primary system is—*pock*—113 minutes. What tools will you require?"

"A standard kit," Wilcox said. "Can I use this one here?"

"Approved."

Pock. Onward.

Kit in hand, he was conducted to a crawlspace above a private room. Below, enclosed in a clear dome as though he were a City in miniature, lay an old man, an old old old man, shriveled and gnomish, cocooned in tubing and spiky cradles of medical apparatus. His face was terribly white, his cheeks were hollow, his eyes were sunken. But those eyes—dark, glistening—peered upward at Wilcox with electric intensity. Trying to ignore the old man's gaze, Wilcox began attaching his clamps and meters so that he could probe for the failed circuitry.

"You," the old man said sharply. "Hey. Who are you?"

"Wilcox. Repairman."

"What are you repairing?"

"The maintenance network of your life-support system," Wilcox said. Already he discerned an irregular tremor in one of the inversion nodes, far down in the lower power uptake. The stupid fixing machines never could see the obvious, could they? "Got just a little problem here," he muttered.

"Am I going to die?"

"Not unless I can't get your maintenance network going soon. But you've got nothing to worry about. I think I've got the trouble tracked down." Wilcox slipped a penetration knob on to the main interlocutory cable and performed a deft catheterisation. Wobbly impulses came bubbling up from his pulsation meter. He scowled. That was the trouble locus, no doubt of it, down there in the inversion node, but could he get the defect isolated and a repair patch implanted in time? The clock was ticking.

From the bed: "You. Boy. How old are you?"

"Twenty-three, sir," Wilcox said, his mouth full of cadmium pins.

"That's not bad. That gives you seventy-two years to get yourself into the fix I'm in. Does it bother you when I talk to you?"

"Not really."

"It does, doesn't it? It distracts you and you can't get your work done. But let's talk all the same. Born in the City, I suppose?"

"Where else?"

"Where else, yes. Yes." A dry, cackling chuckle. "Born in the City, never been outside, right?"

Wilcox decoupled four boosters and stuck his head deep into a humming maze of refrigeration coils. Delicately he diminished the helium phase. When he came up for breath, shaking a little, the old man said, "Never been outside, right?"

"Never."

"Three whole generations, no one been outside. We never dreamed it was going to be like that. A certain degree of separation, yes, but not this total, absolute seclusion."

"Sir, it doesn't bother me when you talk, but you might be tiring yourself, and—"

"You know who I am, boy?"

"No, sir."

"Philip Fontana," the old man said.

"You're a Founder?"

"A Founder, yes. The last one left alive, I think. Unless Davies is still alive. He's dead, isn't he . . . Davies?"

"I believe so," said Wilcox, grappling with busbars.

The old man said, "We thought we were doing something marvelous. Protecting thousands of people against the contamination outside. Let New York have its foulness, yes, let them breathe methane if that's what they wanted, but we—we—our City—under our Dome—boy, do you ever think of going outside?"

"No, sir. The idea doesn't come up."

"Know what would happen if you did?"

"I'd gag and retch, I imagine," Wilcox said, and sent a brilliant arc of light into the faulty node.

"You'd die within hours. Infection, exposure, shock. The bacteria out there, the viruses, the garbage in the atmosphere. It's too filthy out there, too clean in here. That's why no one goes out. We created a metropolis of prisoners, boy, serving life sentences. Do you think we set out to do that? No. No. It simply turned out that way."

"Sir—"

"We didn't plan it at all, boy. We planned everything else, but we didn't plan *that*."

"Sir, your dials are showing a lot of stress. I've got your system on manual override, you know, and I'm not a medic, so if you don't stop exciting yourself I'm going to have to call somebody, and then—"

"All right. I'll be still."

"Please. Yes." Wilcox had the defective node isolated at both ends now. Over his shoulder he said to the fixing machine at his side, "Start sliding that implant toward me."

Pock.

Smoothly he seized the replacement part and positioned it over the defective one. No problem, now. The job would be done with plenty of time to spare.

The old man said, "There's a lesson there. Instead of trying to reshape an unsatisfactory reality, we merely escaped from it. Yes?

Yes? So here we are. Here you are. What a clean little sterile world we've built here. Do you know what I'd do, boy, if I were still running things? I'd start letting air in from outside, a little at a time. I'd start conditioning the City people to tolerate the conditions out there again. And then—another two or three generations, maybe— I'd dismantle the Dome."

"When I click my tongue," said Wilcox to the fixing machine, "pull the bad node up and give me clearance to jam the new implant into place."

Click.

Pock.

"There," Wilcox said. Suddenly his whole testing board was lighted up with checkouts. "That's done. It's all right now, Mr Fontana. The network's functioning again. Good-bye, Mr Fontana." He looked down. The dark eyes were closed. The dials were lolling. "Mr Fontana?" he said.

Pock.

"Did I do something wrong?" Wilcox asked.

Pock.

"It was an excellent repair job," the mellow voice said.

"But the patient died!"

"Coincidental. You were not at fault. Even the best life-support system can sustain an organism that old only so long, after all. You may go now."

Wilcox shrugged. He scrambled out of the crawlspace, dropped off the tool kit, filed his job report, and headed home via transit shaft. The time was 0841 hours. He still had a full day of amusement ahead of him.

The girl was sitting in front of the screen.

"Crazy old man," Wilcox said. "One of the Founders, no less. I fixed his maintenance network. He died anyway. You ready to go?"

"Ready any time."

"Now," he said. And they went off to shoot the grav shafts.

The Artifact Business

The Voltuscian was a small, withered humanoid whose crimson throat-appendages quivered nervously, as if the thought of doing archaeological fieldwork excited him unbearably. He gestured to me anxiously with one of his four crooked arms, urging me onward over the level silt.

"This way, friend. Over here is the Emperor's grave."

"I'm coming, Dolbak." I trudged forward, feeling the weight of the spade and the knapsack over my shoulder. I caught up with him a few moments later.

He was standing near a rounded hump in the ground, pointing downward. "This is it," he said happily. "I have saved it for you."

I fished in my pocket, pulled out a tinkling heap of arrow-shaped coins, and handed him one. The Voltuscian, nodding his thanks effusively, ran around behind me to help me unload.

Taking the spade from him, I thrust it into the ground and began to dig. The thrill of discovery started to tingle in me, as it does always when I begin a new excavation. I suppose that is the archaeologist's greatest joy, that moment of apprehension as the spade first bites into the ground. I dug rapidly and smoothly, following Dolbak's guidance.

"There it is," he said reverently. "And a beauty it is, too. Oh, Jarrell-sir, how happy I am for you!"

I leaned on my spade to recover my wind before bending to look. I mopped away beads of perspiration, and thought of the great Schliemann laboring in the stifling heat of Hissarlik to uncover the ruins of Troy. Schliemann has long been one of my heroes—along with the other archaeologists who did the pioneer work in the fertile soil of Mother Earth.

Wearily, I stooped to one knee and fumbled in the fine sand of the Voltuscian plain, groping for the bright object that lay revealed. I worked it loose from its covering of silt and studied it.

"Amulet," I said after a while. "Third Period; unspecified protective charm. Studded with emerald-cut gobrovirs of the finest water." The analysis complete, I turned to Dolbak and grasped his hand warmly. "How can I thank you, Dolbak?"

He shrugged. "Not necessary." Glancing at the amulet, he said, "It will fetch a high price. Some woman of Earth will wear it proudly."

"Ah—yes," I said, a trifle bitterly. Dolbak had touched on the source of my deep frustration and sorrow.

This perversion of archaeology into a source for trinkets and bits of frippery to adorn rich men's homes and wives had always rankled me. Although I have never seen Earth, I like to believe I work in the great tradition of Schliemann and Evans, whose greatest finds were to be seen in the galleries of the British Museum and the Ashmolean, not dangling on the painted bosom of some too-rich wench who has succumbed to the current passion for antiquity.

When the Revival came, when everyone's interest suddenly turned on the ancient world and the treasures that lay in the ground, I felt deep satisfaction—my chosen profession, I thought, now was one that had value to society as well as private worth. How wrong I was! I took this job in the hope that it would provide me with the needed cash to bring me to Earth—but instead I became nothing more than the hired lackey of a dealer in women's fashions, and Earth's unreachable museums lie inch-deep in dust.

I sighed and returned my attention to the excavation. The amulet lay there, flawless in its perfection, a marvelous relic of the great race that once inhabited Voltus. Masking my sadness, I reached down with both hands and lovingly plucked the amulet from the grave in which it had rested so many thousands of years.

I felt a sudden impulse to tip Dolbak again. The withered alien accepted the coins gratefully, but with a certain reserve that made me feel that perhaps this whole business seemed as sordid to him as it did to me.

"It's been a good day's work," I told him. "Let's go back, now. We'll get this assayed and I'll give you your commission, eh, old fellow?"

"That will be very good, sir," he said mildly, and assisted me in donning my gear once again.

We crossed the plain and entered the Terran outpost in silence. As we made our way through the winding streets to the assay office, hordes of the four-armed, purple-hued Voltuscian children approached us clamorously, offering us things for sale, things they had made themselves. Some of their work was quite lovely; the Voltuscians seem to have a remarkable aptitude for handicrafting. But I brushed them all away. I have made it a rule to ignore them, no matter how delightful a spun-glass fingerbowl they may have, how airy and delicate an ivory carving. Such things, being contemporary, have no market value on Earth, and a man of my limited means must avoid luxuries of this sort.

The assay office was still open, and, as we approached, I saw two or three men standing outside, each with his Voltuscian guide.

"Hello, Jarrell," said a tall man raucously.

I winced. He was David Sturges, one of the least scrupulous of the many Company archaeologists on Voltus—a man who thought nothing of breaking into the most sacred shrines of the planet and committing irreparable damage for the sake of ripping loose a single marketable item.

"Hello, Sturges," I said shortly.

"Have a good day, old man? Find anything worth poisoning you for?"

I grinned feebly and nodded. "Nice amulet of the Third Period. I'm planning on handing it in immediately, but if you prefer I won't. I'll take it home and leave it on my table tonight. That way you won't wreck the place looking for it."

"Oh, that won't be necessary," Sturges said. "I came up with a neat cache of enamelled skulls today—a dozen, of the Expansion Era, set with platinum scrollwork." He pointed to his alien guide, a dour-looking Voltuscian named Qabur. "My boy found them for me. Wonderful fellow, Qabur. He can home in on a cache as if he's got radar in his nose."

I began to frame a reply in praise of my own guide when Zweig, the assayer, stepped to the front of his office and looked out. "Well, who's next? You, Jarrell?"

"Yes, sir." I picked up my spade and followed him inside. He slouched behind his desk and looked up wearily.

"What do you have to report, Jarrell?"

I drew the amulet out of my knapsack and handed it across the desk. He examined it studiously, noticing the way the light glinted off the facets of the inset gobrovirs. "Not bad," he said.

"It's a rather fine piece, isn't it?"

"Not bad," he repeated. "Seventy-five dollars, I'd say."

"*What*? I'd figured that piece for at least five hundred! Come on, Zweig, be reasonable. Look at the quality of those gobrovirs!"

"Very nice," he admitted. "But you have to understand that the gobrovir, while attractive, is intrinsically not a very valuable gem. And I must consider the intrinsic value as well as the historical, you know."

I frowned. Now would come the long speech about supply and demand, the scarcity of gems, the cost of shipping the amulet back to Earth, marketing, on and on, on and on. I spoke before he had the chance. "I won't haggle, Zweig. Give me a hundred and fifty or I'll keep the thing myself."

He grinned slyly. "What would *you* do with it? Donate it to the British Museum?"

The remark stung. I looked at him sadly, and he said, "I'll give you a hundred."

"Hundred and fifty or I keep."

He reached down and scooped ten ten-dollar pieces from a drawer. He spread them out along his desk. "There's the offer," he said. "It's the best the Company can do."

I stared at him for an agonised moment, scowled, took the ten tens, and handed over the amulet. "Here. You can give me thirty pieces of silver for the next one I bring in."

"Don't make it hard for me, Jarrell. This is only my job."

I threw one of the tens to the waiting Dolbak, nodded curtly, and walked out.

I returned to my meager dwelling on the outskirts of the Terran colony in a state of deep dejection. Each time I handed an artifact over to Zweig—and, in the course of the eighteen months since I had accepted this accursed job, I had handed over quite a few—I felt, indeed, a Judas. When I thought of the long row of glass cases my discoveries might have filled, in, say, the Voltus Room of the British, I ached. The crystal shields with double handgrips; the tooth-wedges of finest obsidian; the sculptured ear-binders with their unbelievable filigree of sprockets—these were products of one of the most fertile creative civilisations of all, the Old Voltuscians—and these treasures were being scattered to the corners of the galaxy as trinkets.

The amulet today—what had I done with it? Turned it over to—to a *procurer*, virtually, to ship back to Earth for sale to the highest bidder.

I glanced around my room. Small, uncluttered, with not an artifact of my own in it. I had passed every treasure across the desk to Zweig; I had no wish to retain any for myself. I sensed that the antiquarian urge was dying in me, choked to death by the wild commercialism that entangled me from the moment I signed the contract with the Company.

I picked up a book—Evans, *The Palace of Minos*—and looked at it balefully for a moment before replacing it on the shelf. My eyes throbbed from the day's anguish; I felt dried out and very tired.

Someone knocked at the door—timidly at first, then more boldly.

"Come in," I said.

The door opened slowly and a small Voltuscian stepped in. I recognised him—he was an unemployed guide, too unreliable to be trusted. "What do you want, Kushkak?" I asked wearily.

"Sir? Jarrell-sir?"

"Yes?"

"Do you need a boy, sir? I can show you the best treasures, sir. Only the best—the kind you get good price for."

"I have a guide already," I told him. "Dolbak. I don't need another, thanks."

The alien seemed to wrinkle in on himself. He hugged his lower arms to his sides unhappily. "Then I am sorry I disturbed you, Jarrell-sir. Sorry. Very sorry."

I watched him back out despairingly. All of these Voltuscians seemed to me like withered old men, even the young ones. They were an utterly decadent race, with barely a shred of the grandeur they must have had in the days when the great artifacts were being produced. It was odd, I thought, that a race should shrivel so in the course of a few thousand years.

I sank into an uneasy repose in my big chair. About half past twenty-three, another knock sounded.

"Come in," I said, a little startled.

The gaunt figure of George Darby stepped through the door. Darby was an archaeologist who shared many of my ideals, shared my passionate desire to see Earth, shared my distaste for the bondage into which we had sold ourselves.

"What brings *you* here so late, George?" I asked, adding the conventional "And how was your trip today?"

"My trip? Oh, my trip!" He seemed strangely excited. "Yes, my trip. You know my boy Kushkak?"

I nodded. "He was just here looking for a job. I didn't know he'd been working with you."

"Just for a couple of days," Darby said. "He agreed to work for five percent, so I took him on."

I made no comment. I knew how things could pinch.

"He was here, eh?" Darby frowned. "You didn't hire him, did you?"

"Of course not!" I said.

"Well, I did. But yesterday he led me in circles for five hours before admitting he didn't really have any sites in mind, so I canned him. And that's why I'm here."

"Why? Who'd you go out with today?"

"No one," Darby said bluntly. "I went out alone." For the first time, I noticed that his fingers were quivering, and in the dreary half-light of my room his face looked pale and drawn.

"You went out alone?" I repeated. "Without a guide?"

Darby nodded, running a finger nervously through his unruly white forelock. "It was half out of necessity—I couldn't find another boy in time—and half because I wanted to strike out on my own. The guides have a way of taking you to the same area of the Burial Ground all the time, you know. I headed in the other direction. Alone."

He fell silent for a moment. I wondered what it was that troubled him so.

After a pause he said, "Help me off with my knapsack."

I eased the straps from his shoulders and lowered the gray canvas bag to a chair. He undid the rusted clasps, reached in, and tenderly drew something out. "Here," he said. "What do you make of this, Jarrell?"

I took it from him with great care and examined it closely. It was a bowl, scooped by hand out of some muddy-looking black clay. Fingermarks stood out raggedly, and the bowl was unevenly shaped and awkward-looking. It was an extremely uncouth job.

"What is it?" I asked. "Prehistoric, no doubt."

Darby smiled unhappily. "You think so, Jarrell?"

"It must be," I said. "Look at it—I'd say it was made by a child, if it weren't for the size of these fingerprints in the clay. It's very ancient or else the work of an idiot."

He nodded. "A logical attitude. Only—I found this in the stratum *below* the bowl." And he handed me a gilded tooth-wedge in Third Period style.

"This was *below* the bowl?" I asked, confused. "The bowl is more recent than the tooth-wedge, you're saying?"

"Yes," he said quietly. He knotted his hands together. "Jarrell, here's my conjecture, and you can take it for as much as you think it's worth. Let's discount the possibility that the bowl was made by an idiot, and let's not consider the chance that it might be a representative of a decadent period in Voltuscian pottery that we know nothing about.

"What I propose," he said, measuring his words carefully, "is that the bowl dates from classical antiquity—three thousand years back, or so. And that the tooth-wedge you're admiring so is perhaps a year old, maybe two at the outside."

I nearly dropped the tooth-wedge at that. "Are you saying that the Voltuscians are hoaxing us?"

"I'm saying just that," Darby replied. "I'm saying that in those huts of theirs—those huts that are taboo for us to enter—they're busy turning out antiquities by the drove, and planting them in proper places where we can find them and dig them up."

It was an appalling concept. "What are you going to do?" I asked. "What proof do you have?"

"None yet. But I'll get it. I'm going to unmask the whole filthy thing," Darby said vigorously. "I intend to hunt down Kushkak and throttle the truth out of him, and let the universe know that the Voltuscian artifacts are frauds, that the *real* Old Voltuscian artifacts are muddy, ugly things of no esthetic value and of no interest to—anyone—but—us—archaeologists," he finished bitterly.

"Bravo, George!" I applauded. "Unmask it, by all means. Let the greasy philistines who have overpaid for these pieces find out that they're *not* ancient, that they're as modern as the radiothermal stoves in their overfurnished kitchens. That'll sicken 'em—since they won't *touch* anything that's been in the ground less than a few millennia, ever since this revival got under way."

"Exactly," Darby said. I sensed the note of triumph in his voice. "I'll go out and find Kushkak now. He's just desperate enough to speak up. Care to come along?"

"No—no," I said quickly. I shun violence of any sort. "I've got some letters to write. You take care of it."

He packed his two artifacts up again, rose, and left. I watched him from my window as he headed across the unpaved streets to the liquor-dispensary where Kushkak was usually to be found. He entered—and a few minutes later I heard the sound of voices shouting in the night.

The news broke the next morning, and by noon the village was in a turmoil.

Kushkak, taken unawares, had exposed all. The Voltuscians—

brilliant handicrafters, as everyone knew—had attempted to sell their work to the wealthy of Earth for years, but there had been no market. "Contemporary? Pah!" What the customers wanted was *antiquity*.

Unable to market work that was labelled as their own, the Voltuscians had obligingly shifted to the manufacture of antiquities, since their ancestors had been thoughtless enough not to leave them anything more marketable than crude clay pots. Creating a self-consistent ancient history that would appeal to the imaginations of Earthmen was difficult, but they rose to the challenge and developed one to rank with those of Egypt and Babylonia and the other fabled cultures of Earth. After that, it was a simple matter of designing and executing the artifacts.

Then they were buried in the appropriate strata. This was a difficult feat, but the Voltuscians managed it with ease, restoring the disrupted strata afterward with the same skill for detail as they employed in creating the artifacts. The pasture thus readied, they led the herd to feast.

I looked at the scrawny Voltuscians with new respect in my eyes. Obviously they must have mastered the techniques of archaeology before inaugurating their hoax, else they would never have handled the strata relationships so well. They had carried the affair off flawlessly—until the day when one of the Earthmen had unkindly disinterred a *real* Voltuscian artifact.

Conditions were still chaotic when I entered the square in front of the assay office later that afternoon. Earthmen and Voltuscians milled aimlessly around, not knowing what to do next or where to go.

I picked up a rumor that Zweig was dead by his own hand, but this was promptly squelched by the appearance of the assayer in person, looking rather dreadfully upset but still living. He came to the front of the office and hung up a hastily-scrawled card. It read:

NO BUSINESS TRANSACTED TODAY

I saw Dolbak go wandering by and called to him. "I'm ready to go out," I said innocently.

He looked at me, pity in his lidless eyes. "Sir, haven't you *heard?* There will be no more trips to the Burial Grounds."

"Oh? This thing is true, then?"

"Yes," he said sadly. "It's true."

Obviously he couldn't bear to talk further. He moved on, and I spotted Darby.

"You seem to have been right," I told him. "The whole business has fallen apart."

"Of course. Once they were confronted with Kushkak's story, they saw the game was up. They're too fundamentally honest to try to maintain the pretense in the face of our accusation."

"It's too bad, in a way," I said. "Those things they turned out *were* lovely, you know."

"And the Piltdown Man had an interesting jawbone, too," Darby retorted hotly.

"Still," I said, "it's not as if the Voltuscians were being malicious about it. Our peculiarities of taste made it impossible for them to sell their goods honestly—so it was either do it dishonestly or starve. Weren't we caught in something of the same trap when we agreed to join the Company?"

"You're right there," Darby admitted reluctantly. "But—"

"Just a second, friend," said a deep voice from behind us. We turned to see David Sturges glaring at us bitterly.

"What do *you* want?" Darby asked.

"I want to know why you couldn't keep your mouth shut," said Sturges. "Why'd you have to ruin this nice setup for us? What difference did it make if the artifacts were the real thing or not? As long as the people on Earth were willing to lay down real cash for them, why rock the boat?"

Darby sputtered impotently at the bigger man, but said nothing.

"You've wrecked the whole works," Sturges went on. "What do you figure to do for a living now? Can you afford to go to some other planet?"

"I did what was right," Darby said.

Sturges snorted derisively and walked away. I looked at Darby. "He's got a point, you know. We're going to have to go to another planet now. Voltus isn't worth a damn. You've succeeded in uprooting us and finishing the Voltuscian economy at the same time. Maybe you *should* have kept quiet."

He looked at me stonily for a moment. "Jarrell, I think I've overestimated you," he said.

A ship came for Zweig the next day, and the assay office closed down permanently. The Company wouldn't touch Voltus again. The crew of the ship went rapidly through the Terran outpost distributing leaflets that informed us that the Company still required our services and could use us on other planets—provided we paid our own fares.

That was the catch. None of us had saved enough, out of the fees we had received from the Company, to get off Voltus. It had been the dream of all of us to see Earth someday, to explore the world from which our parent stock sprang—but it had been a fool's dream. At Company rates, we could never save enough to leave.

I began to see that perhaps Darby *had* done wrong in exposing the hoax. It certainly didn't help us, and it was virtually the end of the world for the natives. In one swoop, a boundless source of income was cut off and their precarious economy totally wrecked. They moved silently through the quiet streets, and any day I expected to see the vultures perch on the rooftops. Honesty had been the worst policy, it seemed.

Three days after the bubble burst, a native boy brought me a note. It was from David Sturges, and it said, briefly, "There will be a meeting at my flat tonight at 1900. Sturges."

When I arrived, I saw that the entire little colony of Company archaeologists was there—even Darby, who ordinarily would have nothing to do with Sturges.

"Good evening, Jarrell," Sturges said politely as I entered. "I think everyone's here now, and so we can begin." He cleared his throat.

"Gentlemen, some of you have accused me of being unethical," he said. "Even dishonest. You needn't deny it. I *have* been unethical. However," he said, frowning, "I find myself caught in the same disaster that has overtaken all of you, and just as unable to extricate myself. Therefore, I'd like to make a small suggestion.

Accepting it will involve use of some of the—ah—moral flexibility you decry."

"What's on your mind, Sturges?" someone said impatiently.

"This morning," he said, "one of the aliens came to me with an idea. It's a good one. Briefly, he suggested that, as expert archaeologists, we teach the Voltuscians how to manufacture *Terran* artifacts. There's no more market for anything from Voltus—but why not continue to take advantage of the skills of the Voltuscians as long as the market's open for things of Earth? We could smuggle the artifacts to Earth, plant them, have them dug up again and sold there—and we'd make the entire profit, not just the miserable fee the Company allows us!"

"It's shady, Sturges," Darby said hoarsely. "I don't like the idea."

"How do you like the idea of starving?" Sturges retorted. "We'll rot on Voltus unless we use our wits."

I stood up. "Perhaps I can make things clearer to Dr Darby," I said. "George, we're caught in a cleft stick and all we can do is try to wriggle. We can't get off Voltus, and we can't stay here. If we accept Sturges' plan, we'll build up a cash reserve in a short time. We'll be free to move on!"

Darby remained unconvinced. He shook his head. "I can't condone counterfeiting Terran artifacts. No—if you try it, I'll expose you!"

A stunned silence fell over the room at the threat. Sturges glanced appealingly at me, and I moistened my lips. "You don't seem to understand, George. Once we have this new plan working, it'll spur *genuine* archaeology. Look—we dig up half a dozen phony scarabs in the Nile Valley. People buy them—and we keep on digging, with the profits we make. Earth experiences a sudden interest; there's a rebirth of archaeology. We dig up *real* scarabs."

His eyes brightened, but I could see he was still unpersuaded. I added my clincher.

"Besides, George, someone will have to go to Earth to supervise this project." I looked around the room. "We'll have to pool our cash, won't we, to get a man down there?"

I paused, caught Sturges' silent approval. "I think," I said sonorously, "that it is the unanimous decision of this assembly that we nominate our greatest expert on Terran antiquity to handle the job on Earth—Dr George Darby."

I didn't think he would be able to resist that. I was right. Suddenly, Darby stopped objecting.

Six months later, an archaeologist working near Gizeh turned up a scarab of lovely design, finely-worked and inlaid with strange jewels.

In a paper published in an obscure journal to which most of us subscribe, he conjectured that this find represented an outcrop of a hitherto-unknown area of Egyptology. He also sold the scarab to a jewelry syndicate for a staggering sum, and used the proceeds to finance an extensive exploration of the entire Nile Valley, something that hadn't been done since the decline of archaeology more than a century earlier.

Shortly afterward, a student working in Greece came up with a remarkable Homeric shield. Glazed pottery reached the light in Syria, and Scythian metalwork was exhumed in the wilds of the Caucasus. What had been a science as dead as alchemy suddenly blossomed into a new life; the people of Earth discovered that their own world contained riches as desirable as those on Voltus and Dariak and the other planets the Company had been mining for gewgaws, and that they were somewhat less costly in the bargain.

The Voltuscian workshops are now going full blast, and the only limitation on our volume is the difficulty of smuggling the things to Earth and planting them. We're doing quite well financially, thank you. Darby, who's handling the job brilliantly on Earth, sends us a fat check every month, which we divide equally among ourselves after paying the happy Voltuscians.

Occasionally I feel regret that it was Darby and not myself who won the coveted job of going to Earth, but I reconcile myself with the awareness that there was no other way to gain Darby's sympathies. I've learned things about ends and means. Soon, we'll all be rich enough to travel to Earth, if we want to.

But I'm not so sure I *do* want to go. There was a *genuine* Voltuscian antiquity, you know, and I've become as interested in that as I am in that of Greece and Rome. I see an opportunity to do some pure archaeology in a virgin field of research.

So perhaps I'll stay here after all. I'm thinking of writing a book on Voltuscian artifacts—the *real* ones, I mean, all crude things of no commercial value whatever. And tomorrow I'm going to show Dolbak how to make Mexican pottery of the Chichimec period. It's attractive stuff. I think there ought to be a good market for it.

The Silent Colony

Skrid, Emerak, and Ullowa drifted through the dark night of space, searching the worlds that passed below them for some sign of their own kind. The urge to wander had come over them, as it does inevitably to all inhabitants of the Ninth World. They had been drifting through space for eons; but time is no barrier to immortals, and they were patient searchers.

"I think I feel something," said Emerak; "the Third World is giving off signs of life."

They had visited the thriving cities of the Eighth World, and the struggling colonies of the Seventh, and the experienced Skrid had led them to the little-known settlements on the moons of the giant Fifth World. But now they were far from home.

"You're mistaken, youngster," said Skrid. "There can't be any life on a planet so close to the sun as the Third World—think of how warm it is!"

Emerak turned bright white with rage. "Can't you *feel* the life down there? It's not much, but it's there. Maybe you're too old, Skrid."

Skrid ignored the insult. "I think we should turn back; we're putting ourselves in danger by going so close to the sun. We've seen enough."

"No, Skrid, I detect life below." Emerak blazed angrily. "And just because you're leader of this triad doesn't mean that you know everything. It's just that your form is more complex than ours, and it'll only be a matter of time until—"

"Quiet, Emerak." It was the calm voice of Ullowa. "Skrid, I think the hothead's right. I'm picking up weak impressions from the Third World myself; there may be some primitive life-forms evolving there. We'll never forgive ourselves if we turn back now."

"But the sun, Ullowa, the sun! If we go too close—" Skrid was silent, and the three drifted on through the void. After a while he said, "All right, let's investigate."

The three accordingly changed their direction and began to head for the Third World. They spiraled slowly down through space until the planet hung before them, a mottled bowl spinning endlessly.

Invisibly they slipped down and into its atmosphere, gently drifting toward the planet below. They strained to pick up signs of life, and as they approached the life-impulses grew stronger. Emerak cried out vindictively that Skrid should listen to him more often. They knew now, without doubt, that their kind of life inhabited the planet.

"Hear that, Skrid? Listen to it, old one."

"All right, Emerak," the elder being said, "you've proved your point. I never claimed to be infallible."

"These are pretty strange thought-impressions coming up, Skrid. Listen to them. They have no minds down there," said Ullowa. "They don't think."

"Fine," exulted Skrid. "We can teach them the ways of civilisation and raise them to our level. It shouldn't be hard, when time is ours."

"Yes," Ullowa agreed, "they're so mindless that they'll be putty in our hands. Skrid's Colony, we'll call the planet. I can just see the way the Council will go for this. A new colony, discovered by the noted adventurer Skrid and two fearless companions—"

"Skrid's Colony. I like the sound of that," said Skrid. "Look, there's a drifting colony of them now, falling to earth. Let's join them and make contact; here's our chance to begin."

They entered the colony and drifted slowly to the ground among them. Skrid selected a place where a heap of them lay massed together, and made a skilled landing, touching all six of his delicately constructed limbs to the ground and sinking almost thankfully into a position of repose. Ullowa and Emerak followed and landed nearby.

"I can't detect any minds among them," complained Emerak, frantically searching through the beings near him. "They look just like us—that is, as close a resemblance as is possible for one of us to have to another. But they don't think."

Skrid sent a prying beam of thought on to the heap on which he was lying. He entered first one, then another, of the inhabitants. "Very strange," he reported. "I think they've just been born; many of them have vague memories of the liquid state, and some can recall as far back as the vapor state. I think we've stumbled over something important, thanks to Emerak."

"This is wonderful!" Ullowa said. "Here's our opportunity to study newborn entities firsthand."

"It's a relief to find some people younger than yourself," Emerak said sardonically. "I'm so used to being the baby of the group that it feels peculiar to have all these infants around."

"It's quite glorious," Ullowa said, as he propelled himself over the ground to where Skrid was examining one of the beings. "It hasn't been for a million ten-years that a newborn has appeared on our world, and here we are with billions of them all around."

"Two million ten-years, Ullowa," Skrid corrected. "Emerak here is of the last generation. And no need for any more, either, not while the mature entities live forever, barring accidents. But this is a big chance for us—we can make a careful study of these newborn ones, and perhaps set up a rudimentary culture here, and report to the Council once these babies have learned to govern themselves. We can start completely from scratch on the Third Planet. This discovery will rank with Kodranik's vapor theory!"

"I'm glad you allowed me to come," said Emerak. "It isn't often that a youngster like me gets a chance to—" Emerak's voice trailed off in a cry of amazement and pain.

"Emerak?" questioned Skrid. There was no reply.

"Where did the youngster go? What happened?" Ullowa said.

"Some fool stunt, I suppose. That little speech of his was too good to be true, Ullowa."

"No, I can't seem to locate him anywhere. Can you? Uh, Skrid! Help me! I'm—I'm—Skrid, it's killing me!"

The sense of pain that burst from Ullowa was very real, and it left Skrid trembling. "Ullowa! Ullowa!"

Skrid felt fear for the first time in more eons than he could remember, and the unfamiliar fright-sensation disturbed his sensitively balanced mind. "Emerak! Ullowa! Why don't you answer?"

Is this the end, Skrid thought, the end of everything? Are we going to perish here after so many years of life? To die alone and unattended, on a dismal planet billions of miles from home? Death was a concept too alien for him to accept.

He called again, his impulses stronger this time. "Emerak! Ullowa! Where are you?"

In panic, he shot beams of thought all around, but the only radiations he picked up were the mindless ones of the newly born.

"Ullowa!"

There was no answer, and Skrid began to feel his fragile body disintegrating. The limbs he had been so proud of—so complex and finely traced—began to blur and twist. He sent out one more frantic cry, feeling the weight of his great age, and sensing the dying thoughts of the newly born around him. Then he melted and trickled away over the heap, while the newborn snowflakes of the Third World watched uncomprehending, even as their own doom was upon them. The sun was beginning to climb over the horizon, and its deadly warmth beat down.

The Four

More than a mile of dark sea-water roofed the city. It lay off the Atlantic coast of North America, nestling beneath the waves, cradled by hundreds of atmospheres of pressure. In the official records, the city's designation was Undersea Refuge PL-12. But the official records, like the rest of the landside world, lay blasted and shattered, and the people of Undersea Refuge PL-12 called their city New Baltimore. Eleven thousand was New Baltimore's population, a figure set by long-dead landside authorities and maintained by rigorous policies of control.

The history of New Baltimore stretched back for one hundred thirteen years. Not one of its eleven thousand inhabitants had not been born in the deep, under the laminated dome that was the city's shield. In the ninetieth year of New Baltimore a child had been allotted to the Foyle family, and Mary Foyle was born. And in the hundred thirteenth year of the city—

Mary Foyle lay coiled like a fetal snake in her room at the New Baltimore Social Hall. She lay with feet drawn up, arms locked over her bosom, eyes closed, mouth slightly open. She was twenty-three, blonde, terrible in her wrath. She was not asleep.

At the ninth hour of the day and the second of her three-hour Free Period, she sensed the approach of a visitor, and hatred gathered in her cold mind. Bitterly, she disengaged herself from what she had been doing, and extended a tendril of thought as far as the door. The mind she encountered was weak, pliable, amiable.

Yes, she thought. Roger Carroll, the silly goose.

Roger's mind formed the thought, *Mary, may I come in?* and he had verbalised as far as "Mary, may—" when she darted a hissing prong of thought at him, and he reddened, cut short his sentence and opened the door.

Lazily Mary Foyle tidied her wrappings and looked up at Roger. He was thin, like all men of New Baltimore, but well muscled and strong. He was a year her junior; gifted, like her, with the Powers, but weak of will and flabby of purpose.

"You'll destroy your Powers if you don't give them free play," she thought coldly at him.

"I'm sorry. It was a slip."

She glared bleakly. "Suppose I slipped and blasted your silly mind?"

"Mary, I've never denied that you're more powerful than I am—than all three of us put together—"

"Quiet," she ordered. "The others are coming. Try not to look so much like a blithering fool."

Her mind had detected the arrival of the other two members of their little group. Moments later Roger's slower mind had received the signal, and he added his friendly welcome to Mary's cold one.

Michael Sharp entered first; after him, Tom Devers. They were in their late twenties. In them the Powers had ripened slowly, and Mary had found them out only two years before. Roger had been under her sway for nine years. She herself had first sensed the Powers stirring in her mind fifteen years earlier.

There was a moment of blending as the four minds met—Mary's, as always, harshly dominant, never yielding for a moment the superiority that gave her leadership of the group. The greeting was done with; the Four were as one, and the confines of the room seemed to shrink until it cradled their blended minds as securely as the Dome held back the sea from the buildings of New Baltimore.

"Well?" Mary demanded. The challenge rang out and she sensed Roger's involuntary flinch. "Well?" she asked again, deliberately more strident.

Slowly, sadly, came the response: affirmative from Michael, affirmative from Tom, weakly affirmative from Roger. A slow smile spread over Mary's face. Affirmative!

Roger's mind added hesitantly, "Of course, there's grave danger—"

"Danger adds spice."

"If we're caught we're finished—"

Impetuously Mary extended her mind toward Roger's, entered it, made slight adjustments in Roger's endocrine balance. Currents of fear ceased to flow through his body. Trepidation died away.

"All right," Roger said, his mental voice a whisper now. "I agree to join you."

"All agreed, then," Mary said. Her mind enfolded those of the three lean, pale men who faced her. The borders of the small room grew smaller yet, shrank to the size of Mary's skull, then expanded outward.

Four minds linked to one leaped five thousand feet skyward, toward the crisped and blackened land above.

Mary alone could not have done it. She had tried, and much of her bitterness stemmed from the fact that she had failed. She had sent her mind questing out along the sea-bottom, rippling through the coraled ooze to New Chicago and New London and New Miami and the other domed cities that dotted the Atlantic floor. It was strictly illegal for a Sensitive to make contact with the mind of an inhabitant of another Dome, but Mary had never cared much for what the legal authorities said.

She had reached the other cities of the sea-bottom easily enough—though the effort of getting to New London had left her sweat-soaked and panting—but breaking through to the surface eluded her. Time and again she had sent shafts skyward, launching beams of thought through the thick blanket of water above, striving to pierce the ocean and see the land, the ruined land deserted and bare, the land made desolate by radiation. She wanted to see the sky in its blueness, and the golden terror of the naked sun.

She failed. Less than a thousand feet from the surface the impulse sagged, the spear of thought blunted and fell back. In the privacy of her room she tried again, and yet again, until her thin clothes were pasted to her body by sweat.

That was when she realised she would need help.

It was a bitter realisation. Slowly Mary had sought out those she needed, from the two hundred Sensitives of New Baltimore. Roger she had known for years, and he was as much under her domination as was her hand or her leg. But Roger was not enough. She found

Michael and she found Tom, and when rapport had been
established she showed them what she proposed to do.

Using them as boosters, as amplifiers, she intended to hurl a
psionic signal through the sea to the surface. She could not do it
alone; in series, the four of them might do almost anything.

They lay, the four of them, sprawled on couches in Mary's room.
With cold fury she whipped them together into the unit she needed.
Michael had objected; after all, the penalty for projecting one's
mind beyond the borders of New Baltimore was death. But Mary
had squashed that objection, welded the Four into One, cajoled and
commanded and pleaded and manipulated.

Now, tenuously, the threaded strand of four-ply thought wove
toward the surface.

Mary had seen the tridims projected on the arching screens in
General Hall. She had an idea of what the surface was like, all
blacks and browns and fused glass and gaunt frameworks that had
been buildings. But she wanted to see it for herself. She wanted
direct visual experience of this surface world, this dead skin of the
planet, cauterised by man's evil. Mary had a lively appreciation of
evil.

Upward they traveled. Mary sensed Michael and Tom and Roger
clinging to her mind, helping her force the impulse upward. Eyes
closed, body coiled, she hurled herself to the task.

And the blackness of the water lightened to dark green as the sun-
warmed zone approached. She had not got this far on her earlier,
solo attempts. Now her mind rose with little effort into the upper
regions of the sea, and without warning cleaved through the barrier
of water into the open air.

Michael and Tom and Roger were still with her.

The sight of landside was dazzling.

The first perception was of the sun; smaller than she had
expected, but still an awesome object, glowing high in the metal-
blue sky. White clouds lay under the sun.

New Baltimore was some miles out at sea. Drifting lazily but yet
with the near-instantaneous speed of thought, they moved land-
ward, ready and eager to see the desolation and ruin.

The shock was overwhelming.

Together, the Four drifted in from the sea, searching for the radiation-blackened fields, the dead land. Instead they saw delicate greenness, carpets of untrodden grass, vaulting thick trees heavy with fruit. Animals grazed peacefully in the lush fields. In the distance, glimmering in the sun, low sloping mountains decked in green rose slowly from the horizon.

Birds sang. Wind whistled gently through the swaying trees. It was as if the hand of man had never approached this land.

Can the scars have healed so soon? Mary wondered. Hardly a century since the bombings destroyed the surface; could the wounds have been covered so rapidly? In wonder she guided the multiple mind down through the warm sky to the ground.

They came alight in a grassy field, sweet with the odors of springtime. Mary felt the tingle of awe. Beings were approaching, floating over the grass without crushing it—not the misshapen mutants some thought might have survived on the surface, but tall godlike beings, smiling their welcome.

A surge of joy rippled through Mary and through her into her three comrades. It would not be hard to teleport their bodies up from the depths. They could live here, in this pleasant land, quitting the confines of New Baltimore. She extended the range of her perception. In every direction lay beauty and peace, and never a sign of the destruction that had been.

Perhaps there was no war, she thought. *The landside people sent our ancestors down into the depths and then hoaxed them.*

And for a hundred years we thought the surface was deadly, radiation-seared, unlivable!

For the first time in her life Mary felt no rancor. Bitterness was impossible in this green world of landside. The sun warmed the fertile land, and all was well.

All—

Sudden constricting impulses tugged at the thread of thought by which the four dreamers held contact with landside.

"Mary, wake up! Come out of it!"

She struggled, but not even the combined strength of the Four could resist. Inexorably she found herself being dragged away, back down into the depths, into New Baltimore, into wakefulness.

She opened her eyes and sat up. On the other couches, Michael and Tom and Roger were groggily returning to awareness.

The room was crowded. Six members of the New Baltimore Control Force stood by the door, glaring grimly at her. Mary tried to lash out, but she was outnumbered; they were six of the strongest Sensitives in New Baltimore, and the fierce grip they held on her mind was unbreakable.

"By what right do you come in here?" she asked, using her voice.

It was Norman Myrick of the Control Force who gave the reply: "Mary, we've been watching you for years. You're under arrest on a charge of projecting beyond the boundaries of New Baltimore."

The trial was a farce.

Henry Markell sat in judgment upon them, in the General Hall of the City of New Baltimore. Procedure was simple. Markell, a Sensitive, opened his mind to the accusing members of the Control Force long enough to receive the evidence against the Four.

Then he offered Mary and her three satellites the chance to assert their innocence by opening *their* minds to him. Sullenly, Mary refused on behalf of the Four. She knew the case was hopeless. If she allowed Markell to peer, their guilt was proven. If she refused, it was an equally tacit admission of guilt. Either way, the penalty loomed. But Mary hoped to retain the integrity of her mind. She had a plan, and a mind-probe would ruin it.

Decision was reached almost immediately after the trial had begun.

Markell said, "I have examined the evidence presented by the Control Force. They have shown that you, Mary, have repeatedly violated our security by making contact with other Domes, and now have inveigled three other Sensitives into joining you for a still bolder attempt. Will you speak now, Mary?"

"We have no defense."

Markell sighed. "You certainly must be aware that our position under the Dome is a vulnerable one. We can never know when the madness that destroyed landside"—Mary smiled knowingly, saying nothing—"will return. We must therefore discourage unofficial contact between Domes by the most severe measures possible. We must retain our position of isolation.

"You, Mary, and your three confederates, have broken this law. The penalty is inevitable. Our borders are rigid here, our population fixed by inexorable boundaries. We cannot tolerate criminals here. The air and food you have consumed up to now is forfeit; four new individuals can be brought into being to replace you. I sentence you to death, you four. This evening you shall be conveyed to the west Aperture and cast through it into the sea."

Mary glared in icy hatred as she heard the death sentence pronounced. Around her, members of the Control Force maintained constant check on her powers, keeping her from loosing a possibly fatal bolt of mental force at the judge or at anyone else. She was straitjacketed. She had no alternative but to submit.

But she had a plan.

They were taken to the West Aperture—a circular sphinctered opening in the framework of the Dome, used only for the purpose of execution. An airlock the size of a man served as the barrier between the pressing tons of the sea and the safety of New Baltimore.

The Four were placed in the airlock, one at a time.

The airlock opened—once, twice, thrice, a fourth time. Mary felt the coolness first, Michael next, then Roger, then Tom. Instantly her mind sought theirs.

"Listen to me! We can save ourselves yet!"

"How? The pressure—"

"Listen! We can link again; teleport ourselves to the surface. You've seen what it's like up there. We can live there. Hurry, join with me!"

"The surface," Roger said. "We can't—"

"We *can* live there. Hurry!"

Michael objected, "Teleportation takes enormous energy. The backwash will smash the Dome. A whole section of the city will be flooded!"

"What do we care?" Mary demanded. "They condemned us to death, didn't they? Well, *I* condemn *them*!"

There was no more time for arguing. Their interchange had taken but a microsecond. They were beginning to drift; in moments, the pressure would kill.

Mary made use of her superior Powers to gather the other three to her. Debating was impossible now. Ruthlessly she drew their minds into hers. She heard Roger's faint protest, but swept it away. For the second time, the Four became One. Mary gathered strength for the giant leap, not even knowing if she could make it but not bothering to consider the possibility of failure now.

Upward.

The passage was instantaneous, as the four minds, linked in an exponential series, ripped upward through the boiling sea toward the surface. Toward the green, warm, fertile surface.

Toward the blackened, seared, radiation-roasted surface.

Mary had only an instant for surprise. The surface was not at all as her mind had viewed it. Congealed rivers of rock wound through the dark fields of ash. The sky hummed with radioactive particles. No life was visible.

Mary dropped to her knees in the blistering ash, still warm from the fires of a century before. The heavy particles lanced through her body. *How can this be?* she wondered. *We saw green lands.*

An impulse reached her from Roger, dying of radiation to her left:

. . . fooled you, Mary. Superior to you in one power, anyway. Imaginative projection. I blanked out real image, substituted phony one. You couldn't tell the difference, could you? Happy dying, Mary . . .

She hissed her hatred and tried to reach him, to rip out his eyes with her nails, but strength failed her. She toppled face-forward, down against the terrible deadly soil of Mother Earth, and waited for the radiation death to overtake her.

Hoaxed, she thought bitterly.

Five thousand feet below, the angry sea, swollen and enraged by the passage of four humans upward through it, crashed against the West Aperture of the New Baltimore dome, crashed again, finally broke through and came raging in, an equal and opposite reaction. Above, Mary Foyle writhed in death-throes under a leaden sky.

Precedent

On the second day of the third week since the Terran mission had arrived on Leeminorr, Lieutenant Blair Pickering committed an outrageous crime. Within an hour news of what Pickering had done had percolated back to the Terran base.

There, Colonel Lorne Norden studied the situation very carefully. Norden was commanding officer of the Terran Cultural and Military Mission on Leeminorr. The actions of his men were, ultimately, his responsibility. And since the Leeminorrans were touchy, formalistic, custom-bound people, highly conscious of the presence of Terrans among them, Norden gave the matter of Pickering's behavior particularly careful attention. He would have to make a decision in the case, and he knew clearly and well the consequences of a wrong-headed decision. The Corps kept careful records. There was a considerable body of precedent.

And precedent dictated special handling for the Pickering case.

The incident had taken place shortly before noon—noon, the holiest hour on Leeminorr. Now, it was one-thirty; the midday repose was ended, and Norden knew it would not be long before indignant Leeminorrans arrived to begin filing their formal complaints.

The Terran camp was eight miles outside the town of Irkhiq, a village of perhaps three thousand Leeminorrans, built radially out from their temple. Norden's office was, coincidentally, located in the same relative position to the other Terran buildings as the Irkhiq temple was to the village surrounding it. It had been sheer accident—the masterplan for Cultural and Military outposts dictated the arrangement—but it had worked out well.

Norden himself waited patiently behind his desk for the first delegation to arrive. He was of medium height, but stocky and thick-muscled; for some reason his legs were short and dumpy, but when everyone was seated around a conference table Norden seemed the biggest man in the room. His hands were enormous; his forearms, massive and corded. He had been in the Service nineteen years. This was the eighth world on which he had served. He had taken his degree in Sociometrics at the University of Chicago in 2685, and five years later had won his commission in the Space Service Military Wing.

He made methodical, crisp notations in the log while waiting. Norden was not a man for brooding idly—and, as for developing a strategy to cope with the potentially explosive situation shaping up, he had done that a long time before.

At 1400 sharp his office communicator glowed. Norden reached smoothly for the stud, switched it on, and said: "Norden here. What goes?"

"Five Leeminorrans here to see you, sir. They look disturbed. It's about this Pickering business, I think. Should I send them in?"

"At once."

Norden tidied his desk, swung around in his chair, and waited. After a moment the doorphone buzzed hesitantly, a timid droning sound.

"Come in," Norden said.

Five Leeminorrans entered, single file, their faces grave and severe. They arranged themselves in an open circle, their leader facing Norden, flanked by two of them at each side.

Norden had always felt faintly uncomfortable in the presence of the Leeminorrans. A short man himself, he had learned to feel distrust for taller people—and the Leeminorrans were tall. They stood nearly seven feet in height, magnificent humanoid specimens with powerful-looking shoulders and brawny frames. Five of them, five males, in the discordantly-colored clothing of anger, savage reds shot through with raging violets and blacks. Their arms and legs were bare, allowing view of the superb muscles. The Leeminorrans had oiled themselves, applying the rancid animal fat that gave sheen and glow to their sleek metallic-blue skins.

Ten eyes, red-rimmed and feral, stared at him. Five lipless slitted mouths scowled down. Five angular-featured alien faces glowered at him. There was a long moment of silence in the room.

Five pairs of arms were extended in a ritual greeting: arms out, palms up, then fists clenched, biceps flexed. Impassively Norden watched the muscles bulge. Without rising, he acknowledged the greeting with three crisp, short Leeminorran syllables.

"You are Colonel Norden?" asked the foremost of the Leeminorrans. His voice was deep and big; it rattled in the cavern of his chest a moment before booming forth into the little room.

"I am," Norden said.

"I am Ahruntinok, Guardian of the Truth. I bring greetings from the Overman of Irkhiq, whose chosen representative I am."

Norden nodded. "The Overman is welcome here himself, of course."

"The Overman did not choose to come," replied Ahruntinok stonily. He gestured at his four companions. "I bring with me two priests of the temple, two servants of the Overman. They, too, offer you greetings."

The four flankers bent their knees solemnly, without speaking. Equally silently, Norden nodded response.

The preliminaries over, Ahruntinok glared down at Norden and said, "You have heard of what took place in Irkhiq this morning?"

"Perhaps. I heard what may have been a distorted account of the event. How does the Overman see it, Ahruntinok?"

"As blasphemy," came the flat, cold reply.

"Suppose you tell me what happened," Norden suggested. With a casual gesture of his left hand he flicked on the autotype; it would be important to have a recording of Ahruntinok's statement later, he knew.

The alien squinted suspiciously at the device as it came humming into life, but made no protest. He said, "It was morning in the village, the sun climbing high toward the top of the sky, when your Pickering and his men arrived in the small car you use for riding. They drove through the outer streets of Irkhiq as they do every morning. They passed the temple. It was nearly the moment of noon, when the sun's rays strike the front steps of the temple, purifying it for that day and making it possible for us to enter and pray.

"Several of us were there when Pickering came along. He entered the temple courtyard. He ignored the cries of the priests in attendance and passed over the steps *at the same moment as the rays of the sun*! Then he proceeded to sit on the steps, draw a food-pack from his uniform pocket, and eat. The priests continued to protest, but he paid no attention to them. When he was finished eating, he crumpled his refuse paper and left it where he sat; then he returned to his vehicle and rode away. The temple is polluted. The purification ceremony will take days."

Ahruntinok paused. His face was bleak; his arms were folded, one six-fingered hand grasping each elbow in an aggressive, accusing manner.

"Lieutenant Pickering has committed blasphemy," the alien said. "He must be tried in full court and punished for this, or else the temple's purification will be made much more difficult."

Norden closed his eyes for a moment—and when he opened them, they were hard and searching. "Pickering's in his quarters now. I haven't spoken to him yet. I want to hear his side of this case."

"How long will that take?"

"Are you in a hurry?"

"The people must travel to the next town to pray. We wish to hold the trial tonight and carry out the sentence on him tomorrow. The Festival of Days is coming; Irkhiq would be forever disgraced if our temple were impure at festival time."

"I see. It'll be a quick trial, then. I suppose you have the verdict all prepared, and it's just a simple matter to run through the legal formalities."

"Lieutenant Pickering has committed blasphemy," the alien repeated sonorously. "The penalty for that is severe. And you Earthmen have agreed to abide by the laws of Leeminorr while you remain here. Surely you won't raise any objection to the trial?"

Norden smiled, but it was an unfriendly, business-like smile. "The implication's unwarranted, Ahruntinok. We've bound ourselves by precedent to abide by local law. If a member of this mission has broken the law, we have to let him be tried by

Leeminorran courts. Naturally we're interested in getting a fair trial for our man."

"He will have justice," Ahruntinok said.

"Good. Come back in five hours and see me again. I'll have Pickering ready for you by then."

"Excellent."

The aliens went into the ritual farewell pattern. It took nearly five minutes before they were through flexing muscles, stooping, and praying. Then they turned and left Norden's office.

Norden sat perfectly still for perhaps thirty seconds, reviewing in his mind the conversation just concluded. He would have to report this to Earth, of course. Close contact with home base was an essential characteristic of this sort of work.

And home base would be interested. After four years, another Markin case had finally come up. The Devall Precedent had taken effect: *if an Earthman breaks a law of the planet where he is stationed, the aliens have the right to request trial by their own legal processes.*

Colonel John Devall had put that rule on the books back in 2705, on the planet Markin, World 7 of System 1106-sub-a. Devall had created a precedent, and it was intrinsic to the nature of the Terran missions to alien worlds that precedents be obeyed. Earth had to appear to the lesser worlds who received Earth's aid as an unchangeable, perfectly consistent culture—otherwise, there might be large-scale distrust.

If an Earth mission on one planet behaved in a certain manner, the other Earth missions would have to conform. It was necessary to present unity of objective as a characteristic of Earthmen.

Devall had set a precedent. *And*, thought Norden, *we're stuck with it!*

Strictly speaking, the parallel did not hold true in all respects. The earlier case had been somewhat different.

According to the tapes of the Devall case, a member of the Terran mission to Markin—a Lieutenant Paul Leonards, botanist—had been on a field trip with two other Earthmen. Discovering a secluded grove, they entered it and proceeded to photograph and take samples from any previously unknown botanical specimens.

Suddenly they had been challenged by an armed alien; he attacked violently, ignoring a command by Lieutenant Leonards to lower his spear and explain his actions. When he charged with the spear, the Lieutenant had been forced to kill him in self-defense.

But then complications began when the Earthmen returned to their base. Protesting aliens declared Leonards had entered a sacred grove and had slain the guardian. They demanded the right to try the Earthman by an ecclesiastical court.

It was then that Colonel Devall had made his famous decision. Devall had been an anthropologist, with a competent though undistinguished service record that had seen him lead missions to eleven worlds.

The problem had never come up before in the great Terran aid program. The aliens refused to listen to the argument that Leonards had had no way of knowing he was trespassing on sacred ground, and that he had killed the guardian only in self-defense. Intent had no place in Markin law; only the sheer pragmatic fact of the law-violation itself concerned them, and that had to be requited.

In the end Devall had handed Leonards over for trial, as the aliens requested. Devall had considered the matter long and deeply, and had concluded that in the spirit of fairness this was the only thing he could do. The Terrans lived among the aliens, and, reasoned Devall, they should therefore be bound by their laws.

Luckily, the Lieutenant had escaped serious harm. It had been trial by ordeal, and they had thrown him in a lake and left him to the mercies of two of the dead man's brothers. But he had outswimmed them, reached safety, and thus was declared not guilty.

Norden was familiar with the case. It was classic in the Corps' annals. He had pondered its implications, second-guessed Colonel Devall, thought the thing through with dogged detailed analysis.

And now his turn had come. Lieutenant Pickering of his staff had blasphemed—not accidentally, as had the man on Markin, but knowingly.

The aliens were aware of the Markin affair. They were anxious to try an Earthman.

Well, thought Norden, *they'll get their wish. Pickering is theirs to try. Let them hold us to the Devall Precedent—but they may not like it!*

*

Norden made some log notations, finishing off his weather report
and adding three or four references to general mission progress, on
the several fronts of survey work, anthropological research, and
technological-medical aid. Each mission had a threefold job, and
was staffed to handle it. It carried out an exhaustive botanical and
zoological survey of the planet, taking as many specimens as
possible; it performed cultural research among the inhabitants; and
—on those worlds where the natives would permit it—Terran
experts offered assistance in raising living standards.

At the same time, of course, an assessment of the planet's military
value was made. It was a precautionary move. The galaxy was a
near-infinite place; there was no telling when or from where a
hostile and dangerous race might arrive, and it helped to have a network of friendly allies spread out across thousands of light-years.

Earth had never run across a world that was its equal
technologically or philosophically; whether it was a matter of
earlier evolution or luck along the way was impossible to
determine, but the fact was undeniable that of the several thousand
inhabited worlds visited by the survey teams in the four centuries
since the development of interstellar travel, not one had reached a
cultural level on a plane with Earth's.

An aid program, then, was a logical necessity. But it had to be
handled with tact; sheer altruism was a difficult concept to put
across, at times.

Norden finished his morning's work and restored the log to its
file. Then, closing down the office equipment, he headed out into
the chill Leeminorran afternoon. A bitter wind was blowing,
tossing swept-up gusts of snow about in the compound. Harsh dark
clouds drifted overhead, and far off near the mountaintops, inches
above the horizon, Norden saw the bleak unwarm brightness of
Leeminorr's unfriendly sun.

This was a hard, infertile world. The Leeminorrans were sturdy
people who gloried in exposing their bodies to the elements, whose
philosophy was based on conflict, and whose lives were battle-
studded and tough. This was not a mechanically advanced world;
communication was poor, transportation crude though adequate.

The Leeminorrans recognised the need for the aid the Terrans offered, but they fought hard to maintain their ability and aloofness even while receiving help. An important part of Norden's job was to see to it that the Terran assistance program never began to seem to the Leeminorrans like a distribution of largesse.

He turned off at the communications center. Norden nodded to the signal officer and said, "Has that subradio solidophone contact with Earth come through yet?"

"Just about to call you, sir. Director Thornton's waiting to see you."

"Thanks," Norden replied curtly, and stepped into the green lambency of the solido field.

Director Thornton sat back of a dark-grained bare desk ornamented in the Kauolanii tradition. He was a lean man, well along in years, thin-lipped, tight-faced, with a dry weather-hewn look about him.

He and Norden knew each other well. Norden had served under him on his own break-in cruise, long before Thornton had gone to Rio de Janeiro to take over the all-important post as Director of the Department of Extraterrestrial Affairs. Now Thornton sat poised, unspeaking, unsmiling, waiting to hear what Norden had to say to him.

The Colonel said, "It happened, finally. Another Devall affair."

Thornton smiled emotionlessly. "I had been wondering how long it would take. It's so easy to trespass on territory whose laws we hardly understand. The surprising thing is that this is only the second time."

"The aliens were here to see me not long ago. Naturally they demand the same privilege Devall granted on Markin. It's another blasphemy case."

"Of course," Thornton said. "The Leeminorrans are at the same general cultural-level as the Marks. At that stage they're likely to be highly blasphemy-conscious. When's the trial?"

"Tomorrow, probably. They'll be back to get the man soon. A full report's on its way to you via autotype. It ought to reach you soon."

Thornton nodded. "What action have you taken, Colonel?"

"The man will be handed over for trial—naturally. I don't feel called on to deviate from the Devall Precedent. The aliens expect that kind of treatment."

"Naturally."

"There may be some outcry on Earth, sir. I'd like to request that you refrain from announcing anything about the trial until its conclusion."

Director Thornton looked doubtful. "It's not our usual policy to suppress news, Colonel. Is there some special reason for this request?"

"There is," Norden replied. "I'd prefer to wait until I have more definite data on the problem here." He stared levelly at Thornton and added, "In the sake of preventing future Devall Precedents. My actions will bind all my successors. I'd like to simplify things for them—and help the Leeminorrans at the same time."

Thornton ran his thin fingers along the elegantly-carved rim of his desk a moment or two, considering Norden's request. A smile spread slowly over his features.

"Very well, Colonel. Request granted. I'll maintain a news-curtain over the Leeminorran situation until hearing from you again. Report to me when the trial's over, of course."

"Yes, sir. Thank you, sir."

Norden stepped back out of the fading field. The last he saw of Director Thornton before the solidophone pattern shattered was the director's face, smiling encouragingly. It was not often that Thornton smiled.

Norden pulled his jumper tight around him and stepped out into the chilly wind.

Thornton had understood him—the smile said as much. Now it was Norden's turn to smile.

An organisation such as the Corps operated on precedent. Precedents, then, were not to be broken lightly.

But, thought Norden, there was nothing in the rules against *bending* them a little.

The delegation from Irkhiq was back at sundown, only this time there were six of them. Ahruntinok led the way, striding magnificently into the compound wearing a blazing red cloak twined with vruuk-feathers and tinged with gold; behind him came the two representatives of the priesthood, the two delegates from the secular government, and a sixth figure, gaunt and bowed.

Watching from the window of his office as the group entered the compound, Norden turned his attention particularly to this sixth man. He was old, much older than any of the other five, and yet he still had majesty in his stride even though his shoulders now sloped in and downward, even though his skin had lost the radiant gleam of young warriorhood.

He wore rich robes, draped thickly over his angular body—but his arms and legs were bare, in Leeminorran fashion, and on them Norden could see the welts and scars of a lifetime of combat. He walked slowly, with a steady tread, and held himself proudly erect. *This one was a man, once*, Norden thought. *He knew how to fight.*

The men were gathering around the compound, watching the slow procession with interest. Norden saw Gomez, the anthropologist in charge, surreptitiously snap a tridim shot of the sextet as they stalked past. The sun was down, and night was coming billowing in; the compound lights were on. Above, the tiny splinter of gleaming rock that was Leeminorr's sole excuse for a moon was rising across the sky, beginning its retrograde evening's course.

The thermometer just outside the window read 32°. Not cold, really, but certainly uninviting enough weather—but there was that old alien, looking seventy or eighty or perhaps ninety, strutting up the hill with arms and legs exposed. These were tough customers, Norden admitted admiringly.

The Leeminorrans reached the top of the little rise and gathered there, waiting. Ahruntinok stood facing Norden's two-story residence, staring in; Norden wondered whether the alien could see him, even in the darkness of twilight. He waited; after a moment he saw Reilly, the chief linguist, hesitantly approach the aliens.

They spoke with each other a few moments, with much bowing and gesticulating. Then Reilly detached himself from the group and crossed the clearing to Norden's place.

Norden met him at the door.

"What did they say?"

"They're here to get Pickering," Reilly explained. "But first they want you to come out and greet them. I told them I'd let you know."

"I'm on my way," Norden said. He slipped into his outer jacket and followed the linguist outside. Night was falling rapidly; he felt the cold whipping through him, whistling against his legs. He felt uncomfortable about greeting the aliens standing up: sitting down, he could more than hold his own, but the difference in height of more than a foot discomforted him when they met outdoors.

He reached the group and Ahruntinok offered a ritual greeting. Norden responded.

"The trial will be held tomorrow," Ahruntinok said. "I have brought the judge." He indicated the old man. "Mahrlek, Grand Judge of Irkhiq. He will pass judgment on the Earthman."

The battle-scarred oldster lowered himself in an elaborate bow; Norden did his best to return it, while the five other aliens glowered sourly at him.

"You will give us the man Pickering now," said Ahruntinok when the greeting was concluded. "Tonight he must remain in Irkhiq. Tomorrow will be the trial."

"Where will the trial be held?" Norden asked.

"Irkhiq. Before the temple. The entire village will be present."

Norden was silent for a moment. At length he said, "Of course, other Earthmen can attend the trial?"

Ahruntinok's face darkened. He said, "There is nothing prohibiting their presence. You will not be permitted to interfere with the trial."

"I simply want to watch it," Norden said.

The big alien snorted suspiciously. The old judge stepped to the fore and said, "The night grows cold. Give us the prisoner."

Norden wondered how Devall had faced the actual moment of transfer of possession, when the life of a Terran was given over into alien hands. It must have been a bleak moment for the man.

He turned and caught sight of Sergeant Heong standing some forty feet away, taking down the proceedings with a portable recorder.

"Heong, go get Lieutenant Pickering," Norden ordered crisply.

"Yes, sir."

Leaving the recorder on, Heong set out across the yard on a jog trot toward the officers' barracks, where Pickering had been confined pending resolution of the case. Norden saw the sergeant pounding at the door; then he disappeared within, returning a moment later followed by the bulky figure of Lieutenant Blair Pickering.

The wind swept low over the camp as Pickering appeared. Norden shivered involuntarily; the temperature was beginning its nightly drop. By 2200 or so, the thermometer would be hovering close to zero, and the wind would shriek like a tormented demon all the bleak night.

Heong and Pickering drew near. The lieutenant was in full uniform, braid and all, though he had left off the ornamental blaster. His boots were polished to mirror intensity; he looked fresh and imposing.

For a moment Norden and Pickering eyed each other. Pickering was a big man, with all of Norden's swelling muscularity plus the long legs that should have been his; he stood six-four, big enough by Norden's standards but still nearly half a foot shorter than Ahruntinok. His face was dark and shadowy, craggy-featured, with a thick beak of a nose mounted slightly askew. He had no scientific specialty; he was one of the base's military attachés, one of a complement of six.

The cold air seemed to transmit an electric crackle of tension. Pickering stood stiffly at attention, staring up at the group of aliens. Norden tried to picture him swaggering into town, cavalierly crossing the threshold of the temple at the very moment the seldom-seen purifying rays of the sun were about to strike it, then contemptuously unpacking and eating his lunch in this most sacred of Leeminorran sanctuaries.

It had been an outrage. And Pickering looked hardly contrite as he stood in the whistling wind, jaw set tightly, arms stiff at his sides.

"At ease, Lieutenant," Norden said.

Pickering sullenly let his shoulders slump, his feet slip apart.

"Pickering, I'm placing you in the custody of this group of Leeminorrans. The man in charge is Ahruntinok, who was appointed Guardian of the Truth by the Overman of Irkhiq. Roughly speaking, he's the prosecuting attorney. This gentleman here is Mahrlek, the Grand Judge who'll try your case."

"Yes, sir," Pickering said tonelessly.

"The trial will be held tomorrow. I'll be present at it, Lieutenant. I've reported details of this case to Director Thornton on Earth."

Norden glanced at the aliens. "He's in your hands. What time does the trial begin?"

"Be there at sunup," Ahruntinok said, "if you wish to be present."

Sunup—and, for the second time in history, a human's life lay in the hands of an alien court of law.

Norden had risen at sunup every day of his adult life; this was no exception. The thermometer showed 24°; dawn was breaking over the wall of mountains to the distant east.

He dressed rapidly. The men who were accompanying him had been picked the night before, their names posted on the camp bulletin board; they were dressed and ready early. Norden saw them gathered round a jeep in the middle of the compound, waiting for him.

A quick splash of depilator took care of his stubbly face. He adjusted his uniform, glanced at his watch, and signalled through the window that he was on his way out.

They made the trip virtually in silence, down the winding rutted road that led from the Terran camp to the village of Irkhiq. There were six in the car; Sergeant Heong drove, and along with Norden came anthropologist Gomez, linguist Reilly, Lieutenant Thomas of the Military Wing staff, and Technical Assistant Lennon.

The eight-mile trip ended, finally; the jeep turned off into the broad road that led through town to the temple. The streets were deserted all the way—and for good reason, Norden saw, as they came within sight of the centrally-located temple; the entire village had come out as advertised to see the trial. Three thousand of them, packed tightly together in the square that faced Irkhiq's temple.

The temple was a blocky unpretty building perhaps a hundred feet high, surmounted by an off-center spire. Architecture on

Leeminorr had never amounted to much. The temple opened out on a wide courtyard, and three great stone steps gave access to the inner areas. It was on those steps that Pickering had allegedly blasphemed and committed sacrilege, and it was on those steps that he was being tried.

No one occupied the courtyard behind the steps. The temple was polluted, and until the purification ceremonies were complete no public services could be held there.

Pickering stood between two towering Leeminorran guards. He was still in his uniform—it looked as if he'd slept in it, or if he hadn't been to sleep at all. He needed a shave. His dark craggy face was scowling, but he remained stiffly at attention; his guards were armed with drawn wide-bladed krisses, and they looked willing to use them at any provocation. Both of them topped seven feet. Pickering was oddly dwarfed between them.

Fanning out to the accused man's right and left were two files of bright-clad priests; back of them stood civil police and local functionaries. Three Leeminorrans sat in a little triangle facing Pickering, in an open space some twenty feet square. At the foremost vertex of the triangle sat Mahrlek, the Grand Judge; behind him and to the left was Ahruntinok, Guardian of the Truth, and next to him, resplendent in his robes of state, was the immense figure of Him, the nameless priest-king, the village Overman—He who gave up his name when he assumed his exalted rank, lest demons learn the true name of the Overman and work harm to the village.

The Earthmen rode their jeep as far as possible toward the temple; when the assembled crowd grew too thick to allow further progress, Norden said, "We'd better get out and walk," and they did.

The throng seemed to melt away on both sides of them as they marched single-file inward toward the temple steps. Passing between the rows of huge aliens was like walking through a field of corn in late summer; even the women were six-footers and better.

They reached the trial area. The trio in the clearing sat quite motionless; Pickering might have been a statue on the temple steps.

Suddenly the Overman rose and spread his arms wide, upward,

encompassing the entire group, it seemed. When he spoke, his voice was a pealing basso that rolled out over their heads and seemed to crash against the mountain wall that ringed in the entire Irkhiq district.

> "*Children of light*
> *Children of darkness*
> *Attend here this day*
> *To see justice done.*
> *That which is wrong*
> *Will be made right*
> *That which is soiled*
> *Will be made clean.*
> *Begin.*"

When the final harsh syllable of the invocation had died away Ahruntinok rose. The Guardian of the Truth was nearly the size of the Overman, but he lacked the awesome presence of the other. He said, simply, "The man from beyond the skies has blasphemed. We gather here today to pass sentence on him, to offer him to justice, to cleanse the temple. The white light of justice will prevail."

At Norden's side, Lieutenant Thomas whispered, "I thought this was supposed to be a *trial*, sir. The way these guys are acting, Pickering's guilt's a matter of common knowledge, and they're here to pass sentence!"

Norden nodded. "I'm aware of that, Lieutenant. Leeminorran law isn't necessarily the same as Earth's. But don't worry."

The two files of priests burst into an antiphony now, the right-hand side giving forth a melismatic line of verse, the left-hand side picking it up on the fourth accented syllable and repeating it. It was not quite singing, not quite speech—an elaborate *sprechstimme* that continued for nearly five minutes in close harmony. Pickering stood frozen as the waves of sound washed over him from right and left, as if bathing him.

The prayer ended. Ahruntinok rose again and recited an account of Pickering's crime, phrasing it in a highly inflected antique manner that was probably the legal dialect on Leeminorr. Norden followed it, but with difficulty; if he had not already been familiar with the facts in the case, he might have been hard put to understand what the Guardian of the Truth was saying.

When Ahruntinok was finished the choir of priests responded with another chanted prayer—a monody this time, slow and grave, building to a moody introverted series of minor-key ejaculations. Norden was glad he had ordered Heong to carry a pocket recorder; in all probability this would be their only chance to record this form of Leeminorran musical art.

Norden glanced at his watch. It was 0800—the trial had been proceeding for more than an hour now—and still not a word had been said in Pickering's defense. The Leeminorran concept of legal form was surprising, but not overly so. This was a rugged people; an offender caught in the act was due for a rugged trial.

For a third time Ahruntinok rose. This time the Guardian of the Truth reviewed the nature of Pickering's offense in five or six terse sentences—*for the benefit of the villagers*, Norden thought, *or perhaps for the benefit of us*—and then stepped forward until he was no more than half a dozen feet from the motionless Pickering.

"The temple must be purified. The crime of blasphemy must be washed away. The demon must be driven from this man who stands on the temple steps.

"Prayers and incense will purify the temple. Prayers and incense will cleanse the village of blasphemy. But only the whip will drive out a demon!"

The priests echoed Ahruntinok's last three sentences. It sounded to Norden like nothing so much as a big scene from *Aida*—one where Radames stands accused. Obviously the "trial" had been carefully rehearsed.

The villagers took it up next. "*Prayers and incense will purify the temple! Prayers and incense will cleanse the village of blasphemy! But only the whip will drive out a demon!*"

Norden glanced at Pickering. The condemned man was utterly emotionless; his jaw was set, his lips clamped, as he listened to the exulting outcry.

Ahruntinok said, "I call now upon the Grand Judge of the village of Irkhiq."

Mahrlek rose.

The old man stepped forward into the place vacated by Ahruntinok. He waited—one minute, two, until the tension drew so tight the ground seemed ready to split under the strain. Finally he lifted his hands overhead, holding them rock-steady, and brought them swiftly down.

A shout went up from the populace.

Mahrlek said, "The temple must be purified. The blasphemy must be driven from the air of the village. He who is possessed by a demon must be cured. Let the demon be exorcised. Let the Earthman be driven once around the village boundaries by men with whips."

Norden felt Lieutenant Thomas nudge him sharply. "Sir, that's murder! They'll whip him to death!"

"Quiet," Norden whispered.

Pickering was staring stonily forward. There was even the beginning of a smile on his face.

Norden held his breath. He had coached Pickering well for this moment; if only they had the ritual down straight—!

In a quiet but authoritative voice Pickering said, "I swear by the sun and the sky, by the mountains and by the snow, that there is no demon in me."

His statement was followed by a sudden moment of shocked silence—broken by a gasp of astonishment that became thunderous when multiplied by three thousand throats.

Ahruntinok was on his feet again, his face purpling; all the Guardian of the Truth's calm of a moment before had vanished. "Impossible! Impossible! How can he make such an oath? How can a demon-possessed one swear by the holy and blessed?"

The chorus of priests had disintegrated into a knot of argumentative theologians. A hot buzz of comment drifted from them. Norden smiled in relief; it had gone across, then. The paradox had been hurled forth.

They were all on their feet now—the Overman, the Grand Judge, Ahruntinok—staring at Pickering. The guards at Pickering's sides tightened their grips on their blades, but superstitiously moved several feet away.

The Grand Judge advanced on wobbly legs. He detached the

jewel-encrusted cowl he wore round his neck and extended it nape-first to Pickering.

"Touch your hands to this and repeat what you just said," Mahrlek ordered in a quavering voice.

Pickering smiled bleakly, grasped the Cowl of Justice, and repeated his statement. The old judge ripped the cowl away and hastily tottered back.

Utter confusion prevailed in the trial area. Norden had chosen his steps wisely. He picked this moment to come forward, jostling his way through the horde of open-mouthed villagers, and entered the cleared area.

"As leader of the Earthmen I claim the right to speak on this matter here and now!"

He glanced in appeal at the Overman.

"Speak," the Overman said hoarsely.

"You have given my man trial by your own ways, and you find he is possessed by a demon. But the oath he has just sworn is one no demon could swear. Is this right?"

The trio of Leeminorrans nodded reluctantly.

"The court is thus in doubt. According to your own law, there is only one way this case may be settled now. I call for that method!"

The aliens exchanged glances. "The trial by combat?" Mahrlek asked querulously.

"Yes," Norden said. "The trial by combat, with Pickering fighting the Guardian of the Truth to determine where justice truly lies in this matter!"

The Overman laughed—a welling crescendo of ironic amusement. His face dissolved into a hundred wrinkling laugh-lines; his body shook.

"Your man—against Ahruntinok?"

"Yes," Norden said.

The Overman gestured, and Ahruntinok crossed the clearing to stand facing Pickering. The Guardian of the Truth was six inches taller than the Earthman, and at least a hundred pounds heavier.

"This is amusing," the Overman said. "But justice must be served. Your choice of weapons?"

"Bare hands," Norden said. "Body against body. Fist against fist."

He looked at Pickering, who merely nodded slightly without otherwise indicating reaction.

"Body against body," the Overman repeated. "Fist against fist."

The Grand Judge said, "It will be the simplest way. The Earthman is mad; this will demonstrate it. And the law calls for such a thing."

For a moment the Overman seemed deep in thought; he stood facing Norden like a slumbering volcano, brooding, eyes turned inward. After a long pause he said, "So be it. Ahruntinok will combat with the Earthman Pickering—naked, on the gaming-ground of Mount Zcharlaad. Justice will be served. The defeat of the Earthman will serve to purify and cleanse us. And then we can drive forth the demon who confuses our trial and bedevils us all."

He pointed toward the Guardian of the Truth. "Ahruntinok, is this trial agreeable to you?"

Ahruntinok grinned. "I welcome it."

"And to you, Earthman?"

Pickering shrugged. "I'll fight him," he said, without altering his sullen expression.

"It is decreed, then." The Overman turned to face the throng. "We shall adjourn to the gaming-ground of Mount Zcharlaad!"

It took nearly half an hour for the crowd to disperse. Norden, Pickering, the three high Leeminorrans, and the five other Earthmen remained in a loose grouping around the temple steps, waiting for the mob to break up.

Little was said. The aliens exchanged a few puzzled whispers, but Norden was unable to hear what they were saying. He could bet on it, though: they were wondering how Pickering had been able to confound their theology so thoroughly. Obviously he was demon-possessed, or else he would never have committed his acts of sacrilege—but yet, no demon could have sworn innocence on the cowl of the Grand Judge. It made no sense. Trial by combat was the simplest solution. If Ahruntinok trounced the Earthman, as seemed most likely, then Pickering was guilty of malicious and deliberate acts against the Leeminorran religion, and the beating he would get from Ahruntinok would be ample punishment. But if Pickering should win—

Norden guessed that the Leeminorrans preferred not to speculate about *that* possibility.

He waited, saying nothing. Pickering stood between his two guards, unsmiling. Finally the time to depart came.

Norden left Pickering behind in custody of the aliens, since he was still nominally a prisoner of theirs. He led the way back to the jeep and they piled in, Heong behind the wheel.

As the turbos thrummed into life, Lieutenant Thomas, the Military Wing attaché, swiveled round to look at Norden, who sat in the back.

"Sir?"

"What is it, Lieutenant?"

"Would you mind explaining the facets of this trial to me? I'm afraid I got lost six or seven turns back, when the prosecuting attorney was still yowling for Pickering's scalp. How come you stepped in and demanded this trial by combat thing?"

The Lieutenant was red-faced; he was acutely conscious, evidently, that he was the only man in the jeep without formal scientific training, and it was rough on him to sit there with his ignorance showing.

Norden said, "Would you have preferred it if I'd kept quiet and let them whip Pickering to death?"

"No, sir—but—sir, it's just as bad this way! That alien must be six foot ten, six-eleven, and close to four hundred pounds. It'll be slaughter, sir!"

"You think so? Watch, then," Norden said, grinning. "Pickering's no midget at six-four."

"He is next to that boy, sir!"

"You watch, Lieutenant. I think I know what I'm doing."

There wasn't much that could be said after that. Norden sat quietly, staring through the jeep window at the steadily more forbidding landscape; they were rising through some rocky country now, following the broad back of a large Leeminorran vehicle bulging with townspeople. The Leeminorrans still used internal-combustion engines for their cars; it made an unholy racket.

They wound upward along the mountain path. The ground was covered with a thick layer of snow, and a vicious wind whined down from the sawtooth crests of the upjutting, unforested mountains. It was hard to believe that this was Leeminorran summer; in the winter, in this continent, temperatures rarely rose above freezing, and in the mountains the thermometer stayed between zero and eighty or ninety below for nine months of the year . . . getting as "warm" as freezing for a brief hot spell in midsummer.

Norden reviewed the steps of the trial in his mind. His report would need to be done with care; it was going to be a document given to every Corps trainee to read, along with Colonel Devall's report that preceded it. The reports would make an interesting pair side by side, he thought.

The Norden Precedent. He liked the sound of that.

He smiled. There would be plenty of theological discussing going on tonight in the village of Irkhiq, he thought. Plenty.

In fact, it was going to take more than one evening to get everything straightened around, theologically. The Leeminorrans might even need a brand new theology before Norden got through with them.

The gaming-ground of Mount Zcharlaad was a broad plateau-like area set in an outstretched arm of the sprawling mountain, at an elevation of perhaps five thousand feet. Norden was grateful for that; much higher up, it might have been too rough on Pickering.

A natural amphitheater ringed the site, a shell-like rise in the rock into which seats had been hewn. Now the villagers filed slowly into the seats. A layer of snow covered the gaming-ground itself, and a bitter wind sliced downward from the higher reaches of the mountain chain.

Pickering did not look worried. He stamped his feet a few times against the cold, but otherwise seemed calm, almost *too* calm. It might have been a fatalistic numbness, Norden thought.

Ahruntinok looked elated. The big alien had already stripped down to his fighting costume—a pair of woven briefs and sandal-like buskins—and was loosening up, flexing his huge muscles, swaggering around the outside of the ring, clenching and unclenching his fists. The cold hardly bothered him. His dull-blue skin was glowing healthily, and his features were animated. Norden wondered how many times Ahruntinok had fought here in the gaming-grounds; not a few, he supposed.

The Grand Judge and the Overman stood silently to Norden's side. Their faces revealed little of any thought patterns behind them.

"When does it start?" Norden asked finally.

"Soon," the Grand Judge said. He pointed to the tiny dot that was the sun, hovering just above the crests of the mountains, and said, "The time is not yet right. A few moments more. A few moments more."

Norden walked over to Pickering. "All set, Lieutenant? Feeling all right?"

"Fine, sir."

"The cold won't bother you, now?"

"It may slow me up a little. I'm not worried about it, sir. I can manage."

"I hope so," Norden said. He glanced up at the big man—who seemed so strangely dwarfed by the towering Leeminorrans—and grinned. "Good luck, Pickering."

"Thanks, sir."

The Grand Judge signaled. It was time for the bout to begin.

He stepped forward. In a surprisingly ringing voice, old Mahrlek announced, "Justice now will be served. Ahruntinok, Guardian of the Truth, will meet in combat the Earthman Pickering."

Priests stationed in the first row of seats set up a wailing ululation of a chant. *Ahruntinok's cheerleaders, no doubt,* Norden thought.

Pickering stripped down to fighting costume—shorts and boots, nothing else. No tape on the fists, no gloves, no masks. Just two naked men against each other, in forty-degree weather, with no holds barred. *Justice will be served here today.*

The priestly chanting reached a wild climax, tenors and basses shrieking in utter atonal discordancy on the final three notes.

Then the gaming-grounds became very silent.

"Justice will be served," said the Grand Judge in solemn, sententious tones.

The fighters stepped forward.

Ahruntinok gleamed with oil; his hairless body shone in the faint sunlight, and his muscles stood out against his sleek skin in sharp relief. He was grinning, showing his mouthful of spadeshaped teeth; he stepped toward the center of the gaming area with a wide rolling walk, like a sailor heading downship in a fierce storm.

Pickering was in the center already, and waiting, poised. His unanointed body had little of Ahruntinok's glamor; he looked too pale, too hairy, too squat and clumsy next to the Guardian of the Truth. Ahruntinok moved with the grace of a well-oiled machine; Pickering, with the awkward ponderous notions of an ancient tank. The only sound was the whistling of the wind.

Ahruntinok broke the silence with three quick grunted guttural syllables: a challenge, perhaps, or an invocation, a prayer. Pickering remained silent.

Arms wide, Ahruntinok moved forward.

Norden saw the strategy at once. Ahruntinok intended to make the most efficient use of his half-foot advantage in size and reach, and of his great weight. He was going to hug Pickering to him, draw the Earthman into a bearlike grip and squeeze him into unconsciousness or death.

Ahruntinok's red-rimmed eyes flashed savagely. He advanced toward Pickering, reaching out to gather the Earthman in.

But Pickering had other ideas. He danced forward into the spreading hoop of Ahruntinok's arms and smashed a fist upward at the square chin of the Guardian of the Truth; then he spun away, quickly, slipping beneath the big alien's guard.

Ahruntinok bellowed in anger and whirled on Pickering. A second time the Earthman tiptoed forward and landed a punch, skipping away untouched. Murmurs began to pass through the watching crowd.

The alien had shown no ill effects as a result of Pickering's two punches, but he was angry. He thundered toward the Earthman now, arms flailing, huge fists whistling through the air. Pickering easily avoided one wild swing that would have been fatal had it landed, and cracked his left fist into Ahruntinok's exposed belly. A gust of air escaped from the alien's mouth.

Ahruntinok howled. The warrior's nobility was gone; he reached out desperately with clawed fingertips and managed to scratch six red lines down Pickering's shoulder—but at the same time the Earthman casually slapped an open-handed blow at Ahruntinok's mouth, and a dribble of red blood trickled forth, running down the alien's chin.

Now the crowd was silent again—*frightened* silent.

Pickering exhaled a cloud of white fog and called out to the alien. Ahruntinok whirled; Pickering hit him with a sharp left to the heart followed with a savagely aimed right smash that sent Ahruntinok's head snapping back.

Norden, at the sidelines, felt a sudden burst of exultation.

The bigger they are, he thought—

Ahruntinok was utterly disorganised. He had never been able to get his superb body unhooked and ready for action; Pickering now seemed all about him, lashing him with blows from every direction at once. Ahruntinok was growling angrily, sending panicky swipes in hopes of felling Pickering with a sudden blow, but he was unable to land any.

Pickering was everywhere. The six-inch height differential mattered very little now. One of Ahruntinok's eyes was swelling shut, now; the other was bruised. The alien's thin lips were split. Sweat washed down his massive shoulders and back, mixed with blood.

Ahruntinok was a wrestler, and a fine one. But the first rule of wrestling is that you have to get hold of your man before you can do any damage to him. And Pickering moved too quickly for that.

Ahruntinok was turning in circles, howling like a blinded Polyphemus, imploring Pickering to come within range of his crushing grip. Pickering did—just long enough to detonate an uprising right off the point of Ahruntinok's chin. The giant wobbled; Pickering lifted another from the floor and Ahruntinok staggered forward, still conscious, blood and spittle foaming from his mouth.

Norden glanced at the Overman. He looked sick.

Ahruntinok dropped wearily to his knees and straggled toward

Pickering, groping for him. Pickering ran forward and slapped Ahruntinok twice, fast, to keep him conscious a while longer. The alien rocked and tried to take his feet again; Pickering grabbed one of Ahruntinok's arms and whipped it up suddenly behind the giant's back.

Norden wondered if they'd invented the half-nelson on Leeminorr. If they hadn't, they were in for an enlightening sight now.

With his free arm Ahruntinok vainly tried to catch hold of Pickering, who stood just behind him. Pickering proved uncatchable. He bent Ahruntinok's arm higher, higher, holding it now in an unbreakable grip.

Norden had never heard three thousand more silent people in his life.

Pickering was grinning savagely now. Norden saw that he had absorbed a few bruises in the contest himself; one lip was puffy, and his left ear was swollen. But generally he seemed in good shape. He yanked Ahruntinok's arm up. The giant grunted.

A single loud *crack!* resounded over the gaming-grounds.

Pickering released Ahruntinok's suddenly limp arm and stood back as the giant writhed in pain, knotting his huge legs as if wishing he had Pickering's neck imprisoned between his tightening thighs. Pickering grasped Ahruntinok's other arm and glanced questioningly at Norden.

Norden shook his head.

"No," he said in English. "Enough's enough. Don't break the other one."

Pickering looked disappointed, but he let Ahruntinok's arm drop, and stepped back. The giant lay huddled face down on the hard snow, still conscious but not moving. His great body was racked by three loud, bitter, bewildered sobs. He made no attempt to rise.

—the harder they fall, Norden thought.

Pickering was coming off the battlefield now. He was gasping hard for breath, and his skin was blue and goosepimpled from the cold, but he was traveling under his own steam. He crossed the field, drew near the Overman and the Grand Judge, and sank to the ground at their feet.

Kneeling, he looked up at the Overman and repeated the words Norden had taught him.

"My lord, I ask forgiveness for what I've done. The guilt of blasphemy lies on me still. Will you deign to punish me?"

If Pickering had struck him in the face, the Overman could not have looked more astonished. Mouth open, he stared from the huddled figure of Ahruntinok lying alone in the center of the gaming-ground to the kneeling figure of Pickering. In a hesitant, surprisingly small voice he said, "Punish you? The trial is over, and you have won. How can we punish you now?"

"I insist, my lord. I blasphemed at your temple."

Norden forced back a grin at the Overman's discomfiture. The priest-king was looking at the Grand Judge as if expecting some answer, some way out of this dilemma: how could Pickering have committed blasphemy if the result of the trial-by-combat showed clearly he was innocent? There had been a hundred witnesses to his act. How—?

The Grand Judge, of course, had no answer.

Norden stepped forward. It was not part of his plan to humiliate the Overman before all his village.

He said, "The man is clearly innocent by your law. I ask your permission to take him back, to settle his case among ourselves. May we have him? Will you release him from your custody?"

Something similar to horror passed over the Overman's face. "Yes," he said, much too quickly. "The man's yours. The matter's ended, so far as we're concerned. Take him! Take him!"

But the matter, of course, was far from ended so far as the Leeminorrans were concerned. Their troubles, Norden thought, were just beginning.

He stared at the solidophoned figure of Director Thornton and said, "I did the same thing Devall did, sir. One of my men committed a crime against their laws, they came to me to demand him for trial, and I handed him over to them. You have to admit I was perfectly fairminded about it."

"You were," Thornton chuckled. "Clean and aboveboard in the dirtiest way possible."

"I object! Just because I handpicked my criminal, and just because he *deliberately* committed blasphemy in the most open and casual manner, and just because I knew that Leeminorran law provided recourse to trial by combat if the accused man requested it—"

"—and just because your man Pickering just happened to be one of Earth's most murderous professional boxers," Thornton added—

"Well? The job got done, didn't it?" Norden demanded.

"It did indeed. And very well, too, according to your report. There'll be a commendation for you, Norden. And when you're through with Leeminorr, I'll try to find a less wintry world for your next stop. Seems to me you've had a succession of rough assignments."

"I like it that way, sir," Norden said quietly.

"But—"

"Sir?"

That was all he needed to say.

Later, as he sat alone in his room filling out the routine report on the weather for that day, he paused to think over what he had done.

He felt pretty good about it. He had come to Leeminorr with a purpose, and he had fulfilled that purpose.

He scribbled busily away. *Fifth September 2709. Colonel Lorne Norden reporting. Eighteenth day of our stay on Leeminorr, World Five of System 2279-sub-c. Morning temperature 23 at 0700.*—

The Corps, he thought, had been saddled by the Devall Precedent: when an Earthman commits a crime on an alien world where he's part of a study team, he's responsible to the inhabitants of that world.

Devall had been an intelligent man, but a fuzzy thinker. His line of reasoning was down in his report: *I believed I should treat the aliens as equals, and the best way to prove this equality to them was to subject ourselves to their legal code.*

That was all well and good, thought Norden, as he continued working. There was only one minor hitch: the aliens were *not* equal. It was sloppy-minded to insist that they were.

The Markins had used trial by ordeal; the Leeminorrans, trial by combat. Both good systems, in their day—but not the best. Their results had little to do with actual justice, much as their proponents thought they did.

Norden had fought a double battle, and had won both. He had effectively smashed the Devall Precedent, and he had taught the Leeminorrans a few things about justice.

Simple. Just see to it that your man commits a flagrant abuse of the law in the presence of a few hundred witnesses—and then, when they take him away for trial, have him prove his undeniable innocence *by their laws*. Then let them square the problem of how a man can so obviously commit blasphemy and still get away with it at trial.

That ought to shake a couple of their concepts, Norden thought. It ought to show them a thing or two about the effectiveness of trial by combat. And they'll think twice before they hail an Earthman up before their courts again, too.

He finished writing, closed up, and filed away the log. He walked to the window. Night had fallen; the splinter of moon was overhead, and a light snow was dropping through the cold darkness.

Devall's mistake had been to treat his bunch of aliens as if they were equals, when they really weren't—not *yet*. Norden had shown the Leeminorrans the flaw in the Devall Precedent: if you want to be treated like equals, you have to face the consequences. And the consequences, in this case, proved pretty ugly for poor Ahruntinok.

But he'd recover, and the Leeminorrans would learn something from the incident. Norden smiled.

He liked the sound of it: Norden's Precedent. *If aliens demand equality with Earthmen, give 'em all the equality they can stand. Give it to 'em till it hurts!*

That would hold as a good rule of thumb, Norden thought. Until the race came along that really *deserved* equality, and that was a different matter.

He snapped off the light and headed out into the snow, trotting across the compound to the medical building. The docs were fixing up Pickering, taking the bruises out of him and removing the dent a wild swipe had put in his nose. Pickering had gone through a lot lately, Norden thought. The Colonel wanted to congratulate him for a good job, well done.

After the Myths Went Home

For a while in those years we were calling great ones out of the past, to find out what they were like. This was in the middle twelves—12400 to 12450, say. We called up Caesar and Antony, and also Cleopatra. We got Freud and Marx and Lenin into the same room and let them talk. We summoned Winston Churchill, who was a disappointment (he lisped and drank too much), and Napoleon, who was magnificent. We raided ten millennia of history for our sport.

But after half a century of this we grew bored with our game. We were easily bored, in the middle twelves. So we started to call up the myth people, the gods and the heroes. That seemed more romantic, and this was one of Earth's romanticist eras we lived in.

It was my turn then to serve as curator of the Hall of Man, and that was where they built the machine, so I watched it going up from the start. Leor the Builder was in charge. He had made the machines that called the real people up, so this was only slightly different, no real challenge to his talents. He had to feed in another kind of data, full of archetypes and psychic currents, but the essential process of reconstruction would be the same. He never had any doubt of success.

Leor's new machine had crystal rods and silver sides. A giant emerald was embedded in its twelve-angled lid. Tinsel streamers of radiant platinum dangled from the ebony struts on which it rose.

"Mere decoration," Leor confided to me. "I could have made a simple black box. But brutalism is out of fashion."

The machine sprawled all over the Pavilion of Hope on the north face of the Hall of Man. It hid the lovely flicker-mosaic flooring, but at least it cast lovely reflections into the mirrored surfaces of the exhibit cases. Somewhere about 12570, Leor said he was ready to put his machine into operation.

We arranged the best possible weather. We tuned the winds, deflecting the westerlies a bit and pushing all clouds far to the south. We sent up new moons to dance at night in wondrous patterns, now and again coming together to spell out Leor's name. People came from all over Earth, thousands of them, camping in whisper-tents on the great plain that begins at the Hall of Man's doorstep. There was real excitement then, a tension that crackled beautifully through the clear blue air.

Leor made his last adjustments. The committee of literary advisers conferred with him over the order of events, and there was some friendly bickering. We chose daytime for the first demonstration, and tinted the sky light purple for better effect. Most of us put on our youngest bodies, though there were some who said they wanted to look mature in the presence of these fabled figures out of time's dawn.

"Whenever you wish me to begin—" Leor said.

There were speeches first. Chairman Peng gave his usual lighthearted address. The Procurator of Pluto, who was visiting us, congratulated Leor on the fertility of his inventions. Nistim, then in his third or fourth successive term as Metaboliser General, encouraged everyone present to climb to a higher level. Then the master of ceremonies pointed to me. No, I said, shaking my head, I am a very poor speaker. They replied that it was my duty, as curator of the Hall of Man, to explain what was about to unfold.

Reluctantly I came forward.

"You will see the dreams of old mankind made real today," I said, groping for words. "The hopes of the past will walk among you, and so, I think, will the nightmares. We are offering you a view of the imaginary figures by means of whom the ancients attempted to give structure to the universe. These gods, these heroes summed up patterns of cause and effect, and served as organising forces around which cultures could crystallise. It is all very strange to us and it will be wonderfully interesting. Thank you."

Leor was given the signal to begin.

"I must explain one thing," he said. "Some of the beings you are about to see were purely imaginary, concocted by tribal poets, even as my friend has just told you. Others, though, were based on actual human beings who once walked the Earth as ordinary mortals, and who were transfigured, given more-than-human qualities, raised to the pantheon. Until they actually appear, we will not know which figures belong to which category, but I can tell you how to detect their origin once you see them. Those who were human beings before they became myths will have a slight aura, a shadow, a darkness in the air about them. This is the lingering trace of their essential humanity, which no mythmaker can erase. So I learned in my preliminary experiments. I am now ready."

Leor disappeared into the bowels of his machine. A single pure note, high and clean, rang in the air. Suddenly, on the stage looking out to the plain, there emerged a naked man, blinking, peering around.

Leor's voice, from within the machine, said, "This is Adam, the first of all men."

And so the gods and the heroes came back to us on that brilliant afternoon in the middle twelves, while all the world watched in joy and fascination.

Adam walked across the stage and spoke to Chairman Peng, who solemnly saluted him and explained what was taking place. Adam's hand was outspread over his loins. "Why am I naked?" Adam asked. "It is wrong to be naked."

I pointed out to him that he had been naked when he first came into the world, and that we were merely showing respect for authenticity by summoning him back that way.

"But I have eaten the apple," Adam said. "Why do you bring me back conscious of shame, and give me nothing to conceal my shame? Is this proper? Is this consistent? If you want a naked Adam, bring forth an Adam who has not yet eaten the apple. But—"

Leor's voice broke in: "This is Eve, the mother of us all."

Eve stepped forth, naked also, though her long silken hair hid the curve of her breasts. Unashamed, she smiled and held out a hand to Adam, who rushed to her, crying, "Cover yourself! Cover yourself!"

Surveying the thousands of onlookers, Eve said coolly, "Why should I, Adam? These people are naked too, and this must be Eden again."

"This is not Eden," said Adam. "This is the world of our children's children's children's children."

"I like this world," Eve said. "Relax."

Leor announced the arrival of Pan the Goat-Footed.

Now Adam and Eve both were surrounded by the dark aura of essential humanity. I was surprised at this, since I doubted that there had ever been a First Man and a First Woman on whom legends could be based; yet I assumed that this must be some symbolic representation of the concept of man's evolution. But Pan the half-human monster also wore the aura. Had there been such a being in the real world?

I did not understand it then. But later I came to see that if there had never been a goat-footed man, there nevertheless had been men who behaved as Pan behaved, and out of them that lusty god had been created. As for the Pan who came out of Leor's machine, he did not remain long on the stage. He plunged forward into the audience, laughing and waving his arms and kicking his cloven hooves in the air. "Great Pan lives!" He seized in his arms the slender form of Milian, the year-wife of Divud the Archivist, and carried her away toward a grove of feather-trees on the horizon.

"He does me honor," said Milian's year-husband Divud.

Leor continued to toil in his machine.

He brought forth Hector and Achilles, Orpheus, Perseus, Loki, and Absalom. He brought forth Medea, Cassandra, Odysseus, Oedipus. He brought forth Thoth, the Minotaur, Aeneas, Salome. He brought forth Shiva and Gilgamesh, Viracocha and Pandora, Priapus and Astarte, Diana, Diomedes, Dionysus, Deucalion. The afternoon waned and the sparkling moons sailed into the sky, and still Leor labored. He gave us Clytemnestra and Agamemnon, Helen and Menelaus, Isis and Osiris. He gave us Damballa and Guede-nibo and Papa Legba. He gave us Baal. He gave us Samson. He gave us Krishna. He woke Quetzalcoatl, Adonis, Holger Dansk, Kali, Ptah, Thor, Jason, Nimrod, Set.

The darkness deepened and the creatures of myth jostled and

tumbled on the stage, and overflowed on to the plain. They mingled with one another, old enemies exchanging gossip, old friends clasping hands, members of the same pantheon embracing or looking warily upon their rivals. They mixed with us, too, the heroes selecting women, the monsters trying to seem less monstrous, the gods shopping for worshippers.

Perhaps we had enough. But Leor would not stop. This was his time of glory.

Out of the machine came Roland and Oliver, Rustum and Sohrab, Cain and Abel, Damon and Pythias, Orestes and Pylades, Jonathan and David. Out of the machine came St George, St Vitus, St Nicholas, St Christopher, St Valentine, St Jude. Out of the machine came the Furies, the Harpies, the Pleiades, the Fates, the Norns. Leor was a romantic, and he knew no moderation.

All who came forth wore the aura of humanity.

But wonders pall. The Earthfolk of the middle twelves were easily distracted and easily bored. The cornucopia of miracles was far from exhausted, but on the fringes of the audience I saw people taking to the sky and heading for home. We who were close to Leor had to remain, of course, though we were surfeited by these fantasies and baffled by their abundance.

An old white-bearded man wrapped in a heavy aura left the machine. He carried a slender metal tube. "This is Galileo," said Leor.

"Who is he?" the Procurator of Pluto asked me, for Leor, growing weary, had ceased to describe his conjured ghosts.

I had to request the information from an output in the Hall of Man. "A latter-day god of science," I told the Procurator, "who is credited with discovering the stars. Believed to have been a historical personage before his deification, which occurred after his martyrdom by religious conservatives."

Now that the mood was on him, Leor summoned more of these gods of science, Newton and Einstein and Hippocrates and Copernicus and Oppenheimer and Freud. We had met some of them before, in the days when we were bringing real people out of lost time, but now they had new guises, for they had passed through the mythmakers' hands. They bore emblems of their special functions, symbols of knowledge and power, and they went among us offering to heal, to teach, to explain. They were nothing like the real Newton and Einstein and Freud we had seen. They stood three times the height of men, and lightnings played around their brows.

Then came a tall, bearded man with a bloodied head. "Abraham Lincoln," said Leor.

"The ancient god of emancipation," I told the Procurator, after some research.

Then came a handsome young man with a dazzling smile and also a bloodied head. "John Kennedy," said Leor.

"The ancient god of youth and springtime," I told the Procurator. "A symbol of the change of seasons, of the defeat of summer by winter."

"That was Osiris," said the Procurator. "Why are there two?"

"There are many more," I said. "Baldur, Tammuz, Mithra, Attis."

"Why did they need so many?" he asked.

Leor said, "Now I will stop."

The gods and heroes were among us. A season of revelry began.

Medea went off with Jason, and Agamemnon was reconciled with Clytemnestra, and Theseus and the Minotaur took up lodgings together. Others preferred the company of men. I spoke a while with John Kennedy, the last of the myths to come from the machine. Like Adam, the first, he was troubled at being here.

"I was no myth," he insisted. "I lived. I was real. I entered primaries and made speeches."

"You became a myth," I said. "You lived and died and in your dying you were transfigured."

He chuckled. "Into Osiris? Into Baldur?"

"It seems appropriate."

"To you, maybe. They stopped believing in Baldur a thousand years before I was born."

"To me," I said, "you and Osiris and Baldur are contemporaries. To me and all the people here. You are of the ancient world. You are thousands of years removed from us."

"And I'm the last myth you let out of the machine?"

"You are."

"Why? Did men stop making myths after the twentieth century?"

"You would have to ask Leor. But I think you are right: your time was the end of the age of myth-making. After your time we could no longer believe such things as myths. We did not *need* myths. When we passed out of the era of troubles we entered a kind of paradise where every one of us lived a myth of his own, and then why should we have to raise some men to great heights among us?"

He looked at me strangely. "Do you really believe that? That you live in paradise? That men have become gods?"

"Spend some time in our world," I said, "and see for yourself."

He went out into the world, but what his conclusions were I never knew, for I did not speak to him again. Often I encountered roving gods and heroes, though. They were everywhere. They quarreled and looted and ran amok, some of them, but we were not very upset by that, since it was how we expected archetypes out of the dawn to act. And some were gentle. I had a brief love affair with Persephone. I listened, enchanted, to the singing of Orpheus. Krishna danced for me.

Dionysus revived the lost art of making liquors, and taught us to drink and be drunk.

Loki made magics of flame for us.

Taliesin crooned incomprehensible, wondrous ballads to us.

Achilles hurled his javelin for us.

It was a season of wonder, but the wonder ebbed. The mythfolk began to bore us. There were too many of them, and they were too loud, too active, too demanding. They wanted us to love them, listen to them, bow to them, write poems about them. They asked questions—some of them, anyway—that pried into the inner workings of our world, and embarrassed us, for we scarcely knew the answers. They grew vicious and schemed against each other, sometimes causing perils for us.

Leor had provided us with a splendid diversion. But we all agreed it was time for the myths to go home. We had had them with us for fifty years, and that was quite enough.

We rounded them up, and started to put them back into the machine.

The heroes were the easiest to catch, for all their strength. We hired Loki to trick them into returning to the Hall of Man. "Mighty tasks await you there," he told them, and they hurried thence to show their valor. Loki led them into the machine and scurried out, and Leor sent them away, Herakles, Achilles, Hector, Perseus, Cuchulainn, and the rest of that energetic breed.

After that many of the demonic ones came. They said they were as bored with us as we were with them and went back into the machine of their free will. Thus departed Kali, Legba, Set, and many more.

Some we had to trap and take by force. Odysseus disguised himself as Breel, the secretary to Chairman Peng, and would have fooled us forever if the real Breel, returning from holiday in Jupiter, had not exposed the hoax. And then Odysseus struggled. Loki gave us problems. Oedipus launched blazing curses when we came for him. Daedalus clung touchingly to Leor and begged, "Let me stay, brother! Let me stay!" and had to be thrust within.

Year after year the task of finding and capturing them continued, and one day we knew we had them all. The last to go was Cassandra, who had been living alone in a distant island, clad in rags.

"Why did you send for us?" she asked. "And, having sent, why do you ship us away?"

"The game is over," I said to her. "We will turn now to other sports."

"You should have kept us," Cassandra said. "People who have no myths of their own would do well to borrow those of others, and not just as sport. Who will comfort your souls in the dark times ahead? Who will guide your spirits when the suffering begins? Who will explain the woe that will befall you? Woe! Woe!"

"The woes of Earth," I said gently, "lie in Earth's past. We need no myths."

Cassandra smiled and stepped into the machine. And was gone.

And then the age of fire and turmoil opened, for when the myths went home the invaders came, bursting from the sky. And our towers toppled and our moons fell. And the cold-eyed strangers went among us, doing as they wished with us.

And those of us who survived cried out to the old gods, the vanished heroes.

"Loki, come!"

"Achilles, defend us!"

"Shiva, release us!"

"Herakles! Thor! Gawain!"

But the gods are silent, and the heroes do not come. The machine that glittered in the Hall of Man is broken. Leor, its maker, is gone from this world. Jackals run through our gardens, and our masters stride in our streets, and we are made slaves. And we are alone beneath the frightful sky. And we are alone.